Susan Carlisle's love affair with books began in the sixth grade, when she made a bad grade in mathematics. Not allowed to watch TV until she'd brought the grade up, Susan filled her time with books. She turned her love of reading into a passion for writing, and now has over ten Medical Romances published through Mills & Boon. She writes about hot, sexy docs and the strong women who captivate them. Visit SusanCarlisle.com.

WITHDRAWN

Also by Susan Carlisle

The Doctor's Redemption
His Best Friend's Baby
One Night Before Christmas
Married for the Boss's Baby
White Wedding for a Southern Belle
The Doctor's Sleigh Bell Proposal
The Surgeon's Cinderella
Stolen Kisses with Her Boss
Christmas with the Best Man

Discover more at millsandboon.co.uk.

REDEEMING THE REBEL DOC

SUSAN CARLISLE

MILLS & BOON

Published in Great Britain 2018
by Mills & Boon, an imprint of HarperCollins*Publishers*
1 London Bridge Street, London, SE1 9GF

© 2018 Susan Carlisle

ISBN: 978-0-263-93341-3

MIX
Paper from
responsible sources
FSC
www.fsc.org
FSC™ C007454

This book is produced from independently certified FSC™ paper
to ensure responsible forest management.
For more information visit www.harpercollins.co.uk/green.

Printed and bound in Spain
by CPI, Barcelona

To Jeanie,
I couldn't have asked for a better sister-in-law.

CHAPTER ONE

"RETRACTOR!" SNAPPED Dr. Rex Maxwell.

His surgical nurse quickly placed it in his palm.

"We need to find this bleeder. Suction." With a gentle movement, Rex lifted the liver as his assistant, standing across the OR table from him at Metropolitan Hospital in Memphis, Tennessee, obeyed his command.

Rex watched intently for any sign of red liquid. This patient had come through the emergency department the night before and one of his colleagues had patched the man up but the patient wasn't recovering as he should. His midsection had swelled. There was internal bleeding. Rex was known as the "go-to man" who handled hard-to-find problems like this. He didn't disappoint. Confident in his skills as a surgeon, his success rate had proved him more than competent. Except in one case.

His heart jumped as he spotted the problem. "Found it. Sutures."

"That figures. You find them when no one else can," the anesthesiologist said, admiration in his tone.

Rex looked over his mask at the man. "Thanks."

Over the next few minutes Rex repaired the leak. He was almost finished when the phone on the wall rang. A nurse answered. Seconds later she hung up. "Rex, you're wanted in Administration as soon as you're done here."

He muttered a word that his mother would scold him for using. Polite people didn't use words like that. But, then, to her, life was about always making the right impression.

An hour later he trudged down the wide tiled hallway toward the hospital administration offices. With a patient in surgery prep who had been pushed back hours because of the bleeder, Rex should be back in surgery, not on his way to a meeting he wasn't interested in being a part of. Hadn't he spent enough time in the last twelve months with Dr. Nelson, the hospital administrator? Being arbitrarily summoned to Nelson's office should have stopped when the unpleasant malpractice suit had been settled.

Rex had endlessly replayed the details of that night and that surgery in his mind and had told lawyers the tale of what had occurred more than once.

He'd been called in late on a Saturday night after having been to a club on a date. Since he had been on call he hadn't been drinking and when he'd arrived at the hospital the patient had already been prepped for surgery. It hadn't been until after he was in the OR that he'd learned his patient was Mr. Royster, the man who had been both his father's best friend and chairman of the board of the country club when his father had filed for bankruptcy. Royster was also the father of Rex's ex-girlfriend, who had dumped him because she'd been ashamed of being seen on Rex's arm after his family's financial downfall had become public knowledge.

The situation with Mr. Royster's perforated stomach had by now deteriorated to the point that he'd had little chance of surviving even with surgery. The repair hadn't been difficult but the chance of serious infection had been high. Less than twenty-four hours post-op Mr.

Royster had steadily been going downhill. In another forty-eight, he was gone.

Devastated and grief-stricken to the point that they couldn't accept what had happened, Royster's family had lashed out by filing a malpractice suit against Rex, accusing him of not taking the necessary medical steps to save Royster's life in retaliation for how he and his family had been ostracized all those years ago. Powered by the family's money and influence, the case had gone further than it should have. The most damage had been done by the Roysters' manipulation of the media, which had dragged the hospital into the nastiness.

The relationship between Rex and Dr. Nelson had been contentious at best while the hospital had been faced with the possibility of paying millions in damages. Rex's career, as well as his and the hospital's reputation, would still take years to repair. Thankfully, though, both he and the hospital had come through the experience bruised and battered, and both were still in business. So what could Dr. Nelson possibly want now?

Opening the glass door of the administrative suite, Rex went straight to the assistant's desk. "Marsha, please let Dr. Nelson know I'm here."

She nodded toward a closed door. "Go on in. He's waiting on you."

Relief washed through him. At least he didn't have to waste time waiting. He checked his watch as he entered Nelson's office. He was determined to get to his patient sooner rather than later. As Nelson looked up from his chair behind the desk, Rex closed the door.

Dr. Nelson waved him toward a chair. "I'm glad you could make it on such short notice."

Rex dropped into the seat, elbows resting on his

knees, and looked squarely at Dr. Nelson. "I have a patient waiting."

"I won't keep you long. After the unpleasantness of the last year, the hospital's reputation has taken a hit. The community is left with the impression the hospital doesn't provide quality service."

Without thinking, Rex uttered that foul oath again. Dr. Nelson's eyes narrowed. In turn, Rex straightened in his chair. "Everything about my service is high quality. Was and will be in the future. I'll put my skills up against any surgeon's."

"The question is, does the public believe that?" Nelson countered. "This is a serious situation. I'm sure you've noticed the downward turn in your workload."

"Yes, but I'm still very busy." Rex was confident people would soon forget about the long-drawn-out court case. Especially since it was no longer nightly news. Time was the secret. After all, he'd lived through scandal before and survived.

Dr. Nelson's face sobered. He leaned forward, placing his arms on his desk and clasping his hands. Maybe there was more to this meeting than Rex had originally thought. He gave Mr. Nelson his full attention.

"Because of the situation, the board of directors has decided to bring in a public relations firm to help minimize the fallout. With the hospital accreditation committee planning a visit at the end of the month, we need to bolster public opinion as much as possible. Since you were involved in the lawsuit they want your cooperation in the matter. The idea is that if the public perception of you improves then so will the hospital's and vice versa."

Rex held back a frustrated groan. Nelson must be joking. There wasn't time in his day for PR stuff. Instead of voicing his real opinion, he said, "Do you really think that's necessary?"

"It's not what I think but what the board has decided. However, I agree with them. I expect your full cooperation."

Rex started to open his mouth.

Dr. Nelson raised his hand. "The board knows you're a talented, dedicated doctor. They want to keep you but the hospital's reputation must improve. If you plan to continue working here, I highly recommend you go along with this."

Rex was invested in Metropolitan Hospital. With his surgical skills he could work anywhere, but that wouldn't be enough to get him the promotions he craved and if he were to leave it was highly likely that any hospital he applied to would take a dim view of him, given the malpractice lawsuit, even though he had been legally cleared.

He'd been able to start work at Metropolitan as his own person without the worry of the negative connotations of his family name. He'd been exceptionally successful, despite being what some would call a free spirit. There had been no issues until this recent incident and he didn't anticipate any more problems in his future. His intention was to achieve the position of departmental head in this hospital.

Now he was being pressured into unnecessary PR nonsense with no say in the matter.

Just like when he had been a teen and his family had become the subject of too much outside attention.

After his family's fall from their high-society status, he'd vowed he would never be forced into putting on a façade to impress people. However, it seemed that that was what it was going to take if he wanted to achieve his goals in medicine. Even though experience had taught him that putting a pretty face on an ugly reality could backfire badly.

His mother and father had lived that way. The best clothes, nice cars, private school for their children, big house and membership to an exclusive country club. The problem was that they couldn't afford it. Everything had been outward appearance and no substance. When Rex had been seventeen it had all come crashing down. His parents had been exposed and the family had gone bankrupt.

Reality was a too-small apartment on the other side of town, a ten-year-old car, cheap clothes and no more country club.

Most of Rex's friends had turned their backs on him because they'd no longer had anything in common. What had really hurt, though, had been the girl he'd been in love with ending their relationship. When he'd been snubbed by country club snobs, she'd declared they had no future. He wasn't enough for her. So much for love.

Rex had promised himself then that he'd never judge someone by where they lived or what they drove, neither would he ever put on pretensions of wealth and social status to impress again. He was who he was. People could like him or not. That was one of the reasons he wore a T-shirt, jeans and boots to work. He might be a well-paid physician, but his open, honest lifestyle had nothing to do with his salary, his brain or his skills in the OR. He would not tolerate pretense in his life.

Forcing his attention back to the dilemma Dr. Nelson had just created for him, he decided that during this new PR push he'd just lie low and concentrate on his patients. Refuse to get any more involved than he absolutely had to. He had nothing to prove to anyone and nothing to hide.

The moment Rex sighed, satisfied with his decision, Nelson punched a button and told his assistant to send in Ms. Romano.

Tiffani Romano waited apprehensively in the outer office of the administrator. She'd already seen Dr. Nelson but he'd asked her to wait while he spoke to Dr. Maxwell in private, then he would introduce them.

When her boss at Whitlock Public Relations had asked her into his office and explained that Metropolitan Hospital wanted to hire the firm to improve their image she had been excited that he was putting her in charge of the job. Tiffani saw this as a once-in-a-lifetime opportunity to advance in the company. Success in the campaign would give her the two things she desperately wanted—a promotion that would move her to the corporate office in another city and the chance to no longer encounter Lou, her ex-boyfriend, daily.

The only glitch was that she had no respect for the medical community. She knew from personal experience that doctors were only interested in themselves and cared little about the patients whose lives they ruined instead of healed.

When she'd been a child her father had been crippled in a motorcycle accident and he had lost one leg completely and part of another, condemning him to a wheelchair. The situation had made him a very bitter man. To this day, he insisted the doctors had done nothing to save his lower limbs. With his lack of mobility had gone his desire for life—his only joy to be found at the bottom of a bottle or in the comfort of prescription drugs. These tragedies had been underscored by his sullenness, all making it impossible for him to hold down a job.

Her mother had supported her father's vendetta. Suffering through her father's recovery and attitude about his life, the lawsuit he'd pursued against the physicians and hospital, and having little money, she had been almost as unpleasant as her husband. She'd soon divorced Tiffani's father and the once happy household had changed to one of permanent misery. Nothing had been the same after that fateful day.

Her father still complained about how he had been mistreated. Today he was wasting away at an assisted living home, spending more of his time in bed than out. It made Tiffani miserable to visit him and see him like that, but he was her father and she loved him.

Would Dr. Maxwell, with whom she'd have to work closely, be any different than the doctors who had destroyed her father? From what she had read and seen on the news about the malpractice case, she'd believed Maxwell guilty. Nevertheless, he'd been cleared of all charges. She wasn't surprised. Like all physicians, she was sure he'd played God with someone's life with no thought to what would happen to the patient afterward, or the effects on the family. Her father lived in pain daily because of hasty decisions and half-efforts his doctors had made. Though her father had survived, unlike Maxwell's victim, his life and the lives of his family had been destroyed.

Regardless of Dr. Maxwell's devil-may-care attitude, his surgical success rate was above average. That could be used to her advantage if she could keep him in check long enough to achieve the "you-can-trust-me" crusade she envisioned. Her intense month-long strategy was to boldly make him the face people associated with the hospital. It was an ambitious plan and she had no time for indecisiveness or uncertainty.

She would keep her opinions on the medical field to

herself and convince him that it was in his best interest, and the hospital's, to cooperate with her plans. The board expected positive results and she intended to deliver. Doing so was too important to both her career goals and her sanity.

She gripped the business satchel lying on her lap tighter. The merest hope of never again seeing Lou's smug face fueled her determination. Unfortunately, fate had chosen Dr. Maxwell as the key to making that flickering hope her reality.

A young doctor walked past without glancing at Tiffani and sidled up to Dr. Nelson's assistant's desk. With a warm smile, he asked for permission to see Dr. Nelson.

Tiffani surmised the tall, tan man wearing the green scrubs with cheerfully bright headwear over long dark hair bound at the nap of his neck was her soon-to-be PR project, Dr. Maxwell. Despite her distaste for his profession she couldn't deny that he was attractive. In fact, he might be the most interesting man she had ever seen. She couldn't let herself be distracted by that, though, he was still a doctor.

Ten minutes later, Dr. Nelson's assistant caught her attention and said he was ready to see her. Entering the office with confidence, Tiffani saw Dr. Nelson still seated behind his desk and the doctor in scrubs slumped in a chair with his hands in his lap. She could feel defiance radiating from him even though his expression was professionally polite.

Dr. Nelson stood, arms wide and palms up. "Come in, come in, Ms. Romano. I'd like you to meet Dr. Rex Maxwell."

The doctor had the good manners to stand and extend his hand. His long fingers circled hers. The clasp was firm, warm. His dark brown eyes searched hers intently for a moment before he released her hand.

"Please, both of you, sit down," Dr. Nelson said, taking his seat again.

Tiffani took the chair beside the doctor. He glanced at her before turning those sharp eyes on Dr. Nelson, who said, "I've explained the situation to Dr. Maxwell and he's willing to give you his full support."

Dr. Maxwell shifted in his seat. She glanced at him. His attention seemed focused on a small statue on the shelf behind Dr. Nelson's desk. He didn't look pleased.

The older man continued as if he hadn't noticed. "Both of you are professionals. I know you'll handle this project discreetly. With great aplomb. I expect a report in a week that I can give the board." He paused to look at each of them. "I'm here to help and I look forward to this being a meaningful, productive and very successful project. Please, call on me if there are any issues."

Dr. Maxwell stood, passing behind her chair on his way out. He was already in the hallway before Tiffani could gather her purse and bag. She looked at Nelson but he merely watched as she raced after the most important element to her plan. Her timetable required transforming her ideas into reality right away. That meant immediately getting better acquainted with Dr. Maxwell. He, however, was a good way down the long hall and using a stride she found difficult to match.

She called his name but he didn't slow or even look back as he briskly continued. The rapid tap, tap, tap of her heels echoed off the walls so he had to know she was behind him. As he slowed in front of a closed elevator door she finally caught up and grabbed his arm. To her amazement, he looked surprised to see her and glanced at where her hand rested.

Tiffani released him and said breathlessly, "I've been trying to get your attention since we left Dr. Nelson's office."

"I have a patient waiting." He pushed the button for the elevator again. The doors opened.

"We need to talk. I have plans to implement."

He stepped into the elevator, his gaze meeting hers.

She pursed her lips, hitched her bag strap more securely on her shoulder and stepped aboard just as the door was closing.

His eyes widened. "This is a staff-only elevator."

"Then I'll get off when you do. Right now, I am going to talk to you." She was determined to pin him down to a time they could meet. Timing was everything in this campaign.

He gave her a pointed look. "Ms. Romeo, I don't have time to waste right now."

They faced each other like two bulls in a box. She had no intention of letting this man dismiss her. Meeting his obstinate expression with one of her own, she said tightly, "It is Ms. *Romano*. How soon can you meet with me?"

"I don't know how long this surgery will take. You handle things without me."

The elevator stopped. There was a ding before the doors opened. He almost jumped in his haste to get out. Tiffani didn't hesitate to follow. "So I'm to make the decisions and give you the details?"

He kept walking. "Works for me."

She stayed with him, saying in a stern voice, "This project will only be successful if you play a significant part."

They soon faced closed double doors.

Eyes locked on those doors, he removed his badge

and swiped it over an ID pad as he announced, "Look, I have patients to see. I have neither the time nor the interest in being a part of your PR campaign."

The doors opened. He went through.

She did too. "Dr. Maxwell, Dr. Nelson told me you're willing to give this campaign your full support. Did you lie to him or was he lying to me?"

He stopped so suddenly she almost bumped into his backside. "You can't be in here."

"What?" She didn't understand the abrupt change in the conversation.

"This is the surgery suite. Didn't you read any of the signs?" he asked, as if she were a four-year-old.

"Uh, no, I didn't."

"Are you planning to follow me into the OR?"

"No." She certainly had zero interest in doing that. She'd seen enough gore to last her a lifetime, having had to help care for her father. She had started cleaning and bandaging his wounds while she'd been in middle school.

"It was nice to meet you, Ms. Romano," he said stiffly, before he turned and walked away, dismissing her.

Furious, Tiffani backtracked her way to Dr. Nelson's office. The return trip calmed her and she sighed. Somehow, she had to gain Dr. Maxwell's cooperation. Without Dr. Maxwell there was no successful PR crusade, no promotion and no escaping her past.

Rex had been fairly certain when he'd entered Nelson's office that he wasn't going to like whatever the meeting topic was, and then Nelson had caught him off guard with the stupid PR project. Rex had barely been able to conceal his disgust. He hated being forced to be part of another dog-and-pony show at this point in his life, his career. The hospital would survive the recent bad press, just as he had. All that was needed was time. That was what it had taken after the bubble had burst when he'd been a kid. He'd gotten over the lies and what he had believed about his family. He was a better man, a bluntly honest one, thanks to the experience.

No, participating in a cover-up to make everything squeaky clean was something he refused to do. Shouldn't have to. Proving his abilities as a surgeon was unnecessary. He already knew he was good. The people he'd saved before and after Royster were proof enough.

Late that evening, with his patient doing well, he finally got back to his office. The voice mail light was blinking. Ms. Romano's, stating she would like to meet with him first thing in the morning, was the third message. Rex harrumphed. He'd bet she had no idea that his day started at five thirty. She could figure that out on her own. He didn't feel like dealing with her nonsense.

With her dark hair twisted tightly and her expensive-looking navy blue business suit, Ms. Romano struck him as an uptight bit of fluff. Someone trying to project an aura of authority, with her don't-mess-with-me attitude. The only hint that she might have a softer side had been the glimpse of cleavage in the V of her white silk blouse.

Long ago he'd gotten beyond being impressed by what a person wore. Still, something about Ms. Romano's attire made him think she was trying to make a point to the world. He wasn't interested in being a part of her road to redemption or whatever she was after.

His allegiance lay with the free spirits of the world, those willing to live their lives without worrying about public opinion. Ms. Romano's job alone said she cared too much about what people thought. He'd leave making the hospital look good to her and go on about his business.

The next evening it was well past dinnertime when he finally made it back to his office. Intent on grabbing his jacket, finding a hot meal and going home to bed, he opened the door and froze as he reached for his coat. Ms. Romano sat in one of his two visitors' chairs.

She jerked upright in her seat. The file that had been in her hands fell to the floor, scattering papers everywhere.

Had she been asleep? "Ms. Romano?"

"Uh...yeah." She pushed a loose tendril of hair back from her face. "The cleaning person was coming out when I arrived. I told him you were expecting me."

Rex would have to speak to the housekeeping staff about letting people into his office when he wasn't there. Obviously Ms. Romano didn't mind doing whatever it took to get her way. Ignoring her wasn't going to be as easy as he'd thought.

She bent and started gathering her papers. "You didn't return my calls."

Rex went down on his heels to help her. "I've been here since 2:00 a.m."

Lowering her chin, she said, "I thought you were just dodging me."

Guilt pricked him. Ms. Romano said what she thought. She was honest. He respected that. Continuing to pick up the fallen pages, he was adding them to the growing stack in his hand when he glanced down at one of them and saw his name. He looked at her. "Is this your research portfolio on me?"

Her dark green eyes rose to meet his. "You're an important part of my plan. I need to know all I can about you." She took the papers from his hands and stood.

Rex did as well, snapping, "The hospital should be the focus, not me."

"This is about you too. I can drag you in kicking and screaming but you're still going to be a part of the campaign."

He took a deep breath and exhaled through his nose. "And just how do you plan to do that?"

"As I said before, Mr. Nelson assured me you would cooperate with me." Her obstinate expression didn't waver.

Rex detested her threat of blackmail, but he didn't want Dr. Nelson aware of his determination to take as small a role as possible in this PR nonsense. "Look, I've had a long day. I'm tired and hungry. Can't we do this later?"

"No. We've already lost twenty-four hours. We don't have time to waste."

He let out a deep sigh of disgust and sank into his desk chair. "Then let's get on with it. I'm hungry and need some sleep."

She apparently wasn't in the least bit sympathetic that he'd been at the hospital for eighteen hours.

She placed the folder on his desk in front of her, opened it and sorted papers with precision.

Maybe all he'd be required to do was to listen while she talked. He had naught to contribute, except that he wanted nothing to do with this complete waste of his time and the hospital's resources.

"I need to go over a few things with you so I can make calls first thing in the morning. We have such a small window of opportunity we've got to immediately start pitching ideas to the media."

Rex watched her continue to organize her papers. At this rate, it would be a long month.

"I have some very exciting ideas I want to run by you," she said in a swift, cheerful manner.

Rex knew better than to ask but did so anyway. "Such as?"

"I'd like to do an 'in-your-face' campaign. I want to show the hospital trusts you enough to make you their ambassador. Put it right up front. 'Neither I nor the hospital was guilty of malpractice. You can trust us with all your health needs.'" She pointedly looked at him. "If you gain people's trust then the hospital will be trusted too. It all works hand in hand. I have in mind you doing a couple of medical segments on some morning talk shows. Maybe talk about sports health. Hopefully put an article in *Memphis Magazine*. But time might be against us there." She was talking fast while flipping through her portfolio. "A newspaper ad on Sundays might be very effective. People need to get to know the real you."

The PR woman was in her zone. A sour taste formed in his mouth. She seemed to no longer be aware he sat across from her.

Any hope of not being overly involved was waning fast. He had to put the brakes on this madness. A little louder than necessary, he announced, "People who have met me do know the real me. I have nothing to hide or be ashamed of. I'm not about to rub elbows and smile ingratiatingly at the same people who were burning me at the stake a month ago."

She kept her attention on her file, which was now tightly clenched in her fists. "Yes, you will! Not everyone trusts doctors and hospitals. To have any hope of swaying public opinion in your favor, we need to get the media on our side ASAP."

Rex narrowed his eyes and watched her closely. "So, what's in this for you?"

With a startled jerk, she looked directly at him. "What do you mean?"

"I know why I should be so interested in improving the hospital's rep, and even mine, but why're you so enthusiastic about it?"

She studied him for a moment then said with a harsh note in her tone, "Because it's my job."

Had he hit on something? "It seems to me you're going beyond the call of duty to sit in my office, waiting on me for who knows how long, working overtime on just another job."

"If I pull this off, with your help, I have a real chance at a promotion I really want. Need, in fact."

There was her blunt honesty again.

"I see."

"I'm pretty sure you don't but that isn't the issue." She looked away. "I want to have a couple of billboards put up around town. Have people see that the hospital is here for them and that you are part of what makes it… great." She faltered on the last word. As if she weren't sure it was the correct one.

"Me?"

"I want you on the billboard, standing in front of a picture of the hospital. With a healthy, happy patient. You know that kind of thing." She absentmindedly waved one hand in the air.

Rex's insides tightened. His hunger had vanished. This was starting to sound like what his parents had done when he'd been a kid. Make their family look all perfect on the outside. He turned his head to the side and looked down his nose at her. "You want my picture on a billboard?"

"That's right."

He shook his head. "No."

"We need to put you out there in front of the public. Let them know who you really are."

Rex leaned back in his seat and crossed his arms. "I don't think me being on a billboard is going to tell them anything."

Her expression was stony. "Dr. Nelson thought it was a good idea."

She was playing hardball again. Rex felt the walls closing in. He was being left no choice. If he wanted to keep his job, or any chance of becoming department head anytime soon, he would have to go along with this. But he wouldn't make it easy. "I don't have time for these extracurricular activities. My surgical practice and responsibilities to my patients monopolize my time."

"We'll work around your schedule."

His refusal, his objection hadn't even slowed her down.

She studied him a moment. "One more thing. We need to work on your image."

His gut tightened. This was getting worse by the minute. "What's wrong with my image? My appearance is part of my identity."

After looking him over for a moment, she answered in a quiet but steely voice, "You have a bad-boy image. One that has to be softened up a little bit."

"And just how do you plan to do that?"

"A haircut here, some clothes there."

This was going too far. "Not going to happen. I don't do makeovers. You can talk to Nelson all you want but that's stepping over the line."

She slipped the now organized papers into her folder. "After this campaign, you can go back to your slouchy, unkempt look, but you *will* look sharp and reliable for the media. You think about it. From what I understand, this is all sanctioned by the board. I'm not telling you your business but can you really afford to go against them?"

He hated this. Everything about it brought back memories he'd thought he had gotten beyond. "Again, where do I find time for this makeover to happen?"

"Don't you have a day off?" She sounded as if it wasn't a big deal for him to get away.

Yeah, but not one he wanted to spend her way. "Tomorrow, in fact."

"Perfect. I'll make an appointment with my hairdresser for tomorrow afternoon. First we'll do a little shopping. So, I'll be on my way. Goodnight." She stood, put her bag over her shoulder and turned toward the door.

"Hey, wait a minute. You don't need to be going to your car alone at this time of night." Rex picked up his jacket.

She had stopped and was looking back at him. "I'll be fine. I'm in the main parking lot up front."

"I'm still going to walk you out."

She shrugged and walked away. He followed. They said nothing to each other as they went down in the elevator and stepped out into the parking lot. The silence wasn't so much uncomfortable as it was mutual.

"This is it," she said when they reached a white compact car. With a click, she unlocked it with her fob. "Why don't you get in? I'll take you to your car."

Rex wavered a moment, fearing that if he managed to get his long body in he might not be able to get it out. "My bike is in the back. I don't mind walking."

"You ride a motorcycle?" The unusual high note in her voice irritated him.

"Yes. You mean that wasn't in your notes?"

Her perplexed demeanor was almost comical. Had she really thought that everything there was to know about him was in black and white in her folder? "Actually, it wasn't, but it should have been."

He was tired of being under the microscope. First the malpractice suit and now this. He liked his motorcycle. Liked the freedom. The lack of restriction. The fact that he was snubbing people like the ones in his past social circle made it even more fun. "Is me riding a bike a problem?"

"It could be," she said, as if pondering the issue, climbing in and closing her car door, leaving him with the unfortunate feeling he had just become the dog in her dog-and-pony show.

CHAPTER TWO

WHERE IS HE? Tiffani asked herself more than once as she paced in front of the men's store in downtown Memphis. She had texted Rex the address and the time earlier that morning. He'd sent a terse response.

I'll be there when I can.

She hadn't heard another word from him since and his scheduled appointment time with her hairdresser was growing ever closer. Moreover, her father was expecting her later this afternoon. He'd worry if she was late. Rex needed to hurry.

It wouldn't have surprised her, though, if Rex was keeping her waiting on purpose. Wasn't that what doctors did? Made people wait? It proved what she thought about them must be true—little worry for how they affected others—and so Rex not being courteous enough to tell her he'd be late shouldn't have astonished her.

Fuming over her assumption that he'd show up at the time she'd told him, her hopes rose at the roar of a motorcycle. Was that him?

He'd made it clear he didn't like any of her ideas, but she wasn't sure he understood the big picture. He kept insisting he wanted nothing to do with the effort to improve the hospital's reputation. Then he'd flat out balked at her insistence he needed a makeover. Something deep was behind his protests and stubbornness. What had he said about his appearance? He'd said it was part of his identity.

She watched the motorcycle rider pull into a parking spot not far from hers. He wore a plain black T-shirt, worn jeans with a hole in one knee and black ankle-high boots. When he pulled his helmet off, dark hair fell around his broad shoulders. Rex was impressive in a wild sort of way. She almost regretted insisting his hair be cut. Somehow it made him more fascinating. Her opinion, though, didn't matter. What mattered was his image in the eyes of the residents of this city if her plans were to succeed.

Her gaze met his.

"What's wrong?" he asked.

Had she been staring? She went on the defensive. "I expected you here thirty minutes ago. Maybe your patients understand you not showing up on time but I don't."

Climbing off his bike, tucking his helmet under his arm, he stepped into her personal space, claiming all the air around her. She could hardly breathe, let alone hear him quietly inform her, "Something came up at the last minute but I'm here now."

Tiffani took two steps back and inhaled. "You could've at least texted me."

"I didn't have a chance. Sorry. My patient was having difficulty breathing. I didn't have time to message you before I started operating, repairing her lung. Afterward I was too busy rushing here to text you."

She'd firmly been put in her place. Somehow sorry didn't cover it but she said it anyway.

"Now that I'm here, let's get this over with." With a grim look on his face he looked at the storefronts.

"The manager is waiting for us." She led the way to the specialty men's shop.

"I still don't understand why all of this is necessary." He followed close behind her.

Over her shoulder she replied, "That biker gang look might work just fine in your everyday life but in my world a more professional appearance is called for."

"What if I want nothing to do with your world?" Stepping ahead of her, he opened the door.

His manners couldn't be faulted. At least that area needed no work. As she passed him she retorted, "Right now, you have no choice."

He said softly, "We'll see about that."

The middle-aged store manager greeted them and directed them to a row of suits.

"I'd rather not." Rex shook his head. "If I must dress up, I'd prefer jackets and jeans."

"You need a suit. I have a TV interview set up for next week." The opportunity to show Rex as qualified and trustworthy was too good to pass up.

"No suit. It's non-negotiable." The firmness in his tone stated he meant every word.

"You don't make the rules here."

"I do about what I wear," he shot back. "I won't be dressed up and paraded around like a preening bird. Complain to Nelson if you like."

She took a deep but discreet breath, counting to three before she said in her most soothing tone, "We'll try it your way, but I get the final say. If I don't like the look you choose then you may have to try on a suit."

"Won't happen." He turned back to the manager and started pointing at jackets. "I'll try that one, that one and that one." Moving to a wall with cubby holes filled with stacked shirts, he pulled out several. "Here," he said, piling them in her arms. Moving to a rack of pants, he sorted through them until he had chosen a handful. The manager took the pants from Rex, who all but growled, "Where's the dressing room?"

"This way, sir," the older man said, appearing perplexed.

"Just call me Rex."

The man nodded and led the way to the back of the store.

Tiffani followed, feeling a little dazed. Rex had taken over. She needed to regain control but was unsure how to do it.

Rex dropped his helmet on top of the last display table before the dressing stall. Immediately he pulled his shirt over his head.

Tiffani was given a spectacular view of his back muscles shifting under bronzed skin. That expanse of pure masculinity tapered down to a trim waist.

Her step faltered.

Surely it was from the shock of him stripping so freely. Not from the delicious view she'd been given. She should want nothing to do with men, doctors in particular, but she wasn't immune to a good-looking male. Rex Maxwell had a very fine body to go with his handsome face. If he affected her this acutely, surely other women would also be attracted to him. Smiling to herself, she nodded. Tiffani would use his raw virility to her advantage during the campaign.

"Hand me the shirts and pants first. I'll try the jackets on last," he said from behind a wooden door that stopped a couple of feet from the floor. She watched with a skip of a heartbeat as his jeans puddled around his feet.

The manager hurried to give him the pants. Rex opened the door far enough to take them. Seconds later he opened it again and stuck out a hand. "Shirts?"

The manager moved out of Tiffani's way so she could hand him her armload of shirts. She did her best to keep her eyes off the almost naked man before her. When Rex chuckled softly, she instinctively met his gaze. The twinkle in his smoldering eyes made her discomfort intensify. He was playing with her. But she had endured enough cat-and-mouse games for a lifetime.

She quickly turned but not before her downward glance had registered his navy sport briefs barely concealing his manhood. Trying to hide her sexual attraction, she said in as flat a voice as she could muster, "Let me see you when you're dressed."

Minutes later he came out wearing a light blue shirt and navy pants. The manager held up a tan jacket. Rex slipped it on with a grace Tiffani couldn't ignore. He'd been toying with her earlier. Had known he was embarrassing her. Yet here she was, ogling him again. Whatever was going on with her body had to stop. He was a client and one she was determined not to like or trust. All doctors were self-centered and so far Rex Maxwell hadn't proved himself any different.

He put his arms out and slowly turned around. "What do you think? Will I do?"

She studied him intently, hoping to find a flaw. There wasn't one. So she promptly ordered, "Let's see the others."

"No. You can choose what you like out of my selection. I'm done here." He shrugged off the jacket.

She stepped in front of him, ignoring the garment he held out. "You need to try them all on. I want to make sure they create the right image."

He took the stance of a man in a gunfight, letting the jacket sweep the floor when he lowered his arm. His stare was hard. "They're all the same size, just different colors. Mix and match 'em. I've done all the fashion-show stuff I'm going to do. Period."

Everything about him warned she shouldn't push any further. So she looked down at his boots. "Okay. Now for shoes."

Rex lifted a foot, moving it one way then another. "What? You don't think these go with everything?"

Relieved his mood had mellowed, she retorted, "I think traditional footwear would be more appropriate. The boots work for your motorcycle but I don't think they're the best choice for TV interviews or social situations."

"Social situations? What social situations am I going to be in?"

She could feel the appalled aura envelop him.

"The hospital is planning a small cocktail party and dinner for the accreditation committee. It'll be a great opportunity for you to talk to influential members of the community, while impressing the committee. Let them get to know you." She smiled, hoping to encourage him.

His jaw tensed. "I won't be attending. That isn't my thing."

Time to try coaxing. "Sure you will. You'll be the face of the hospital by then. The surgeon everyone wants."

"If that happens it'll be because I'm a great surgeon, which by the way I am, and not because you dressed me up and paraded me around." He headed toward the dressing room.

She called to his back, "It'll be good for you and the hospital."

Rex turned and confronted her. "I have no interest in

being linked to the hospital forever. I've agreed to help because Dr. Nelson strongly encouraged it, but with this I draw the line. I don't do social."

"Your social appearance might mean getting top marks from the accreditation committee. You know they're overly conscious of the malpractice case. We're trying to rebuild some public goodwill as well." She couldn't back down on this. It was the cornerstone of her plan.

"Do you really believe changing my wardrobe and showing me off to people who value appearance over substance is going to make that much difference?" There was a snide tone to his words.

She fervently hoped so. This project was her ticket out of town and away from Lou. "I make a living seeing that it does."

He leaned close and looked her directly in the eyes. "Don't you think honest people see beyond all your publicity? I know I'm more interested when I get to know the real person, not the one putting on shiny shoes and a smile, trying to be someone they're not."

Stepping closer and lowering her voice, she hissed, "You need the shiny shoes and smile so people will want to take the time to get to know you. Do you think black T-shirts, holey jeans and biking boots exude medical professionalism? It's important the community has confidence in you. Believes they'll get the quality of care they expect."

Surprise and then something she wasn't sure she could name flickered in the depths of his eyes. He said, just as quietly, "Their quality of care hasn't changed. Mine or the hospital's. Just because a family wouldn't accept I couldn't save their father's life doesn't mean my skills are any less competent or professional than they were before the malpractice suit."

Tiffani flinched. This conversation was treading too close to the personal. She had promised herself that she would see this job through without letting what had happened to her father intrude. The only way to do that was to go on the defensive. "Just what is your issue? After all, you're getting a new wardrobe at the hospital's expense and you're an intelligent man, so you know how important what I'm trying to achieve is. Why all the pushback?"

"Like I can't afford my own shoes and my own clothes," he spat. "Clothes I have no interest in wearing."

"I still don't understand the problem. It looks to me like you'd want to help." Why couldn't he just not fight her on this?

"The problem is, I'm not going to pretend to be somebody else." He dropped the jacket on a stack of causal shirts and gestured toward the clothes she and the manager still held. "I'm a skilled surgeon, regardless of what I wear. I don't care who is or isn't impressed by my appearance."

She believed him. He was his own man and he was brutally honest. Unlike virtually all the people around her. She had to admire that about him.

After Lou's lies she appreciated the honesty. She was glad that, with Rex, she was certain she wouldn't misread his feelings. He would make them clear. In an odd way, it was refreshing.

But his stubborn insistence that his appearance ought not matter to people would be the ruin of her campaign if she couldn't make him see reality. With his biker appearance came negative connotations, no matter what type of person he really was. With secret desperation she coolly asked, "If you won't present the image the public has of a gifted, confident, trustworthy surgeon, just how do you expect to convince them you *really are* gifted, confident or trustworthy?"

He gave her a seething glare. "And you think this dog-and-pony show you have planned will do that?"

Tiffani raised her chin and shrugged with all the indifference she could muster, sensing victory. "It's done all the time."

Rex seemed at a loss for words. Abruptly she was aware of the manager's intense interest in their disagreement. What was going on between her and Rex wasn't good PR. Taking a cleansing breath, she tried to appease Rex into compromising. "It's just for a little while. I'll try to make it as easy as possible."

"I don't care how long it is. I won't pretend to be somebody I'm not. Ever again."

Again? So there *was* something in his past driving his illogical refusal to admit she was right. "Then I'll make an effort not to ask you to. Agreed?"

Juggling her armload of clothes, she extended her hand. He looked at it for a moment then took it. Inexplicably, a shiver went up her spine at his touch. She pulled her hand free.

"Agreed." His voice was calm and sincere.

She smiled. He was going to try to meet her halfway. Tiffani made her tone appeasing. "Now, I know you don't want to hear this but it's time we get to your hair appointment."

His lips puckered and jaw tightened. Was another fight coming?

To her surprise, he finger-combed his hair back from his face and said, "Okay. But only because I'm due for a trim." He picked up the jacket and returned to the dressing room.

Relief washed through her. The tightness between her shoulder blades eased. A least he was going to go along with her plans regarding his hair. Trim? She needed him to have more than that. She'd let Estell handle making that happen.

While waiting for Rex, she made arrangements with the manager to pick up the purchases later. As they left the store she announced, "The shop isn't far from here. Should we walk?"

"Do you think biker boots will be okay for that?" he asked with a smug smile, tucking his helmet under his arm.

She glared. "Yes, but I don't think they're suitable for every occasion. The hairdresser is this way."

Rex, although familiar with this area of Memphis, had spent little time there. As he examined the small businesses with cute storefronts he noted many of the other people on the street were fashionably dressed and clearly wealthy. It all reminded him too much of his childhood where nothing had mattered but where you shopped and what brand you could afford.

The boutiques lining the street looked just like the ones his mother used to frequent. But then the terrible truth had come out.

At least now he didn't care what he wore as long as it was comfortable. He'd spent half his life going in one direction and the other half hell-bent on another. No way was he returning to the old lifestyle his parents had pretended they could afford. He had no reason to prove himself to anyone through his appearance, zero interest in outside trappings. He knew with bone-deep certainty who he was and for the rest of his life there would be no more pretentious facades.

Still, damn it, he had agreed to help with Tiffani's PR nonsense. His plans for his future actually rested on it to a certain degree. If a few wardrobe changes and a haircut could gain him what he wanted, then was it such a big deal?

Yes! It was a very big deal. He had set his boundaries all those years ago for very real, vital reasons and had successfully, happily lived by them ever since. He had no intention of ignoring them now. Not for Tiffani. Not for anyone. Nor for any reason, regardless of its appeal.

But walking down the street on a sunny day with a pretty woman beside him somehow made all the ridiculousness of this makeover less disturbing to his peace of mind. He glanced at Tiffani. She still wore her hair up but not quite as tightly as before. Her attire was more casual as well. A simple purple knit shirt, black pants and flat shoes unleashed her subtle sex appeal, which floated around her like honeyed perfume.

He didn't care for her high-handed ways and wasn't even sure he liked her, but it was a nice change to argue with someone who gave as good as she got. Few people in his life dared to talk back to him. He'd found his disagreements with Tiffani invigorating, something he'd experienced rarely with a woman. The women he tended to date were only interested in a good time or were in awe of what he did for a living. There was no challenge. Tiffani was definitely that. She wasn't impressed by his looks and certainly not by his position.

They stopped in front of a store with flowers painted on the windows and a sign above the door that read Cute Cuts. He felt his eyes involuntarily roll in disbelief. Maybe he should have ridden his bike and parked it out front. Letting out a low groan, he informed her, "I'm going to have to give up my man card if I go in here."

"It won't be all that bad. I promise." A bell tinkled as she pushed the door open. "Come on in, be brave."

Rex didn't miss the humor in her voice. "It's not courage I lack but desire."

A woman with short, spiked green hair tipped in red looked away from the client she was working on and said to Tiffani, "Hey, girl, I'm almost done here. I'll be right with you."

Rex gave Tiffani a speculative look. She shrugged in response. What had he gotten himself into? This place looked nothing like his barbershop. Instead of a group of balding men sitting in the back, talking and playing checkers, there was a rock station blaring on the sound system and an over-the-head hair dryer going.

The only place to sit in the tiny place was a wicker settee with floral printed cushions.

Tiffani settled on it. Unsure if the wicker was strong enough to hold them both or if he wanted to sit so close to her, he chose to stand.

"She'll be done in a sec, I'm sure," Tiffani offered. "Estell's the best in town."

Rex nodded, but really didn't care. He just hoped one of his male colleagues didn't see him leave the place. The jokes would never end. Had Tiffani been polite enough to ask, he'd have preferred to have gone to his regular guy. Rex's urge to leave grew. Too much of his day off had already been wasted.

Soon the customer was gushing over her new look and leaving.

"I'm ready," Estell called.

He approached her with a tentative smile.

"Well, hello, handsome. What can I do for you today?" Estell purred, low and throaty.

Rex chuckled, liking the "out there" woman. It surprised him that Tiffani used her as her hairdresser. Estell seemed too eccentric to appeal. Tiffani acted so closed off and all business. Was there another side of her he'd not seen?

While he pondered her, Tiffani said, "Estell, I was thinking cut it above the ears. A little longer on the top—"

"I can handle this," Rex stated in his "surgeon-in-OR" voice that tolerated no argument. "Why don't you go get us some drinks? We're good, aren't we, Estell?"

Grinning, she nodded. "Yeah, Tiffani, we're good."

"I need him to look professional, clean cut." Tiffani looked concerned, almost as if she was unsure they could be trusted to be left alone.

"Will do," Estell said, and returned to her cutting chair.

Rex pulled from his pocket a few bills and handed them to Tiffani. "I'd like a soda. Get yourself one too. How about you, Estell?"

She grinned. "Sure."

"Make that three," he added.

Tiffani stood immobile, looking rather bewildered.

He winked. "Take your time. Estell and I might be busy a while."

Estell snickered. Tiffani's eyes narrowed. She muttered as she left, "I don't know about this."

Estell had just finished with his hair when Tiffani returned. With the turn of the chair he faced her as she crossed the threshold. She stopped short, gaping. Heat simmered through Rex. He knew well the pleasure of a woman's admiration, but he'd never experienced one devouring him with her eyes. He shifted uncomfortably as hot blood-hardened parts made themselves known.

"So, what do you think?" Estell asked from behind him.

Tiffani blinked, appearing to struggle back to the here and now. "Uh, I wanted it…much shorter."

"I didn't," Rex announced, his gaze still locked with hers as he slipped out of the chair.

A long second later she fluttered her eyelids. "Okay."

He took the plastic bag she held. Checking its contents, he pulled out a soda and tossed it to Estell, who caught it neatly. He handed Tiffani one before withdrawing and opening his.

As if coming out of a daze, Tiffani straightened her back and glared at him. "You had me go buy these to get rid of me."

Shrugging his shoulders Rex set his drink down and pulled his wallet out. He paid Estell, giving her a generous tip along with a kiss on her cheek. With a wink, he said in a confidential tone Tiffani could hear, "You know what's said at the beauty parlor stays at the beauty parlor."

Tiffani snorted behind him.

Estell giggled and replied, grinning, "I had fun too. Nice to meet you, Rex."

"I'll wait for you outside," he told Tiffani as he stepped around her.

Tiffani wasn't sure what had just happened. She rarely ogled men, especially not one who was her client. Or one she considered egotistically self-absorbed, not to mention argumentative. Yet she'd been literally unable to take her eyes off Rex when she'd reentered the beauty shop. He was gorgeous. All virile male at ease in a den of feminine décor. Confidence oozed from him. To make matters worse, like an idiot she hadn't been able to put two words together.

Estell had taken a few inches off his hair and tamed it around his face so that it complemented his rugged features. It looked healthy and free, just like he was. Tiffani had never been a big fan of men with long hair, but Rex was a definite exception. Her first instinct had been to touch it, to caress his scalp and let the strands flow through her fingers. A totally inappropriate impulse for a professional such as herself.

The worst thing about those first agonizing moments had been his obvious relish of the effect he was having on her. Enjoying it. She mustn't allow that to happen again. She had to remain in control of the situation, and herself, at all times around him. That was the plan.

"Honey." Estell shook her head as if thinking, *Yum, yum, yum.* "You've got a real man on your hands. I hope you can handle him."

"He's not my man. We're business associates." Tiffani almost snapped, wincing at the edge of defiance she heard in her voice. She wasn't interested in a relationship. And certainly not with someone like Rex Maxwell. Her breakup with Lou had guaranteed she'd think long and hard about allowing herself to become intimately involved with another man. Besides which she didn't need one. Heartache was all the opposite sex offered.

"Well, if it was me, I'd sure figure out a way to make him mine," Estell said as she opened her drink.

Rex was standing by a light pole when Tiffani joined him outside. Virtually every female walking by gave him a second look. Obviously, Tiffani's reaction to the new Rex wasn't unique. His image on the billboards would certainly captivate most women. An ambassador who was a handsome surgeon with sex appeal practically assured a positive rise in the hospital's reputation. She was tickled. The campaign was fast becoming far more effective than she'd first hoped. The only thing that might ruin it was Rex inexplicably fighting her every step of the way.

He shifted impatiently from one foot to another. "Is there a café or something around here?"

"Yes, there's one just around the corner." She pointed up the sidewalk.

"Would you like to join me?" Rex asked.

"I guess so." Tiffani didn't make a habit of socializing with clients but she couldn't think of a good excuse not to. She was hungry and had time for a quick meal before she had to leave to see her father. Plus, she had one more thing she needed to discuss with Rex. He'd be more receptive to it if he heard her proposal with a full stomach.

He fell into step beside her. "The women I dine with usually sound more eager to share my company."

"This isn't a date," Tiffani retorted, a little more stiffly than intended. "And I only have time for something quick." She felt his dark eyes on her.

"You have a problem with dating?"

"No," she said slowly. "And you are my client."

He stopped. She did too and looked back at him. People walked around them. He said, as if choosing his words carefully, "And if I wasn't your client? How would you feel?"

"I don't do business and pleasure in the same place." She'd more than learned her lesson there.

"That was a loaded statement. Care to elaborate?"

"I do not. It's too long and too ugly a story." And too humiliating to repeat. Especially to a man who probably never had a female turn him down. "And it has nothing to do with us. The PR campaign, I mean."

"They say talking it out with someone makes it better." He continued along the sidewalk.

She couldn't believe his arrogance. Did he really think confiding in him was going to make anything better? He was a doctor. One she didn't trust. And definitely not a confidant she'd trust her embarrassment to.

"I know you're very sure of your bedside manner but do you really believe I'd spill my life story to you?"

"Not really. But it sounds like it might be interesting."

She looked at her reflection in the glass front of the restaurant. "You should save your charm for the TV interviews."

"Now you're trying to ruin my meal." He opened the door to the small sixties retro café.

They were shown to a table for two in the middle of the dining room and handed menus. After studying the menu, Rex asked, "Anything you can recommend?"

"I've only been here a couple of times. The pork chop and potatoes or the spaghetti is good."

He nodded sagely. The waitress took their drink orders on her way to another table. After a moment he questioned, "Have you decided?"

In principle, sharing social time with a client wasn't a good idea, but the raw truth was that being seen with a good-looking man gave a much-needed boost to Tiffani's damaged ego. Being told you're not wanted by someone she'd thought had loved her had been devastating. After that catastrophe, having any male attention was like a much-needed salve.

Against her better judgment, her mind started to chew over her past love life. Learning Lou didn't return her love had nearly destroyed her. To make matters worse, he'd made a show of announcing to their coworkers that he wanted nothing more to do with her. Had arrogantly declared he was now available during an office meeting. Tiffani had wanted to melt under the table. She'd never been more mortified. In her despair, she'd vowed never again to share herself completely with a man. All the males in her life had always wanted more from her than they had ever been willing to give in return.

The waitress returned with their drinks and took their orders. Tiffani settled on a salad and Rex asked for a pasta dish. With that done, Tiffani said, "I wanted to let you know that I have a photographer coming tomorrow to take pictures of you."

"I have surgeries planned."

"I know. I got your schedule from Dr. Nelson. We'll work around it. The photographer will be at the hospital to take pictures so he can shoot you between your cases."

Rex thumped his fork on the table. "You have to be kidding."

The noise accompanying his disbelieving tone startled her. If she showed weakness now, she feared all would be lost. "Dr. Nelson said we could use a conference room to take formal portrait shots of you."

"You've got it all worked out, haven't you?"

She could tell by the way he clenched his jaw that he was holding back what he would like to say. "It's my job."

"I don't think much of it." His words were heavy with contempt.

She looked him straight in the eyes. "The feeling is mutual."

"How's that?" He looked confused.

"It doesn't matter. We don't have to like each other, or

each other's professions. We just have to work together long enough to repair the hospital's public reputation."

Crossing his arms on the table, Rex leaned toward her. "You expect me to accept that cryptic explanation?"

"You don't get a choice." She took a swallow of her drink and let the ensuing silence between them speak for itself. Thankfully the waitress brought their food in short order. They said little as they ate.

"Someone, help!" cried a woman on the other side of the room. "She's choking."

Tiffani's eyes jerked in the direction of the desperate plea. Even as she did so, Rex shoved his chair back and hurried to the distressed woman, who was beating a child's back, dodging tables as he went. Tiffani followed.

"I'm a doctor. Let me have her," Rex commanded with unquestionable authority.

The woman stopped her movement in midair and handed the gasping child to him.

Rex took the girl's arm and turned her round, pressing her back against his chest. He wrapped his arms around her, clasping his fists together and positioning them under her ribs before giving her a tight squeeze.

Nothing happened. The girl's lips were turning bluer.

Rex pulled the girl tight again and landed an audible blow to her abdomen. Something popped from her mouth. The child gasped, taking deep breaths. The mother descended on her, crying and pulling her from Rex's hold into a tight hug.

Clutching her daughter, she raised a tear-streaked face to Rex. "Thank you, thank you, thank you."

His smile was one of relief. "You're welcome. What's your name?" he asked the girl.

"Lucy."

"Lucy, I'm Dr. Rex. Will you let me give you a little check just to make sure everything's all right?"

The elementary-school-aged girl gave her mom a questioning look. The mother nodded, her sobs subsiding.

"Why don't you have a seat right here?" Rex asked, pulling out a chair.

Tiffani couldn't deny he was good. She shouldn't have been surprised. After all he was a charmer. It occurred to her that this was the type of stuff she couldn't manufacture with billboards and TV interviews.

"I'm going to sit right here." Rex pulled up a chair in front of the girl, ignoring the other patrons crowding around them. "Why don't you open your mouth and let me have a look?"

The girl did as he requested.

He unclipped his keys from the belt loop of his jeans. There was a small penlight on the ring. Turning it on, he examined the girl's throat. "Looks good in there. I'm going to check your neck. Tell me if it hurts."

The girl nodded.

"That was pretty scary, wasn't it?" Rex said to the child as his fingers worked over the outside of her neck.

This was PR that Tiffani couldn't pass up. She had been terrified for the child but now that the drama was over she had to think about her job. This was perfect material. Dr. Rex, The Respectable Good Samaritan. She hurried back to their table and pulled her phone from her purse. Seconds later she was taking pictures of Rex and the girl. Maybe some of the others had gotten video of him saving her.

He glanced up at her, his eyes narrowed, before his attention went back to the girl.

Tiffani continued taking pictures.

"Take a deep breath for me," Rex said to Lucy. She inhaled and exhaled. "I think you're going to be just fine," he pronounced, and stood.

The mother hugged him. "Oh, thank you. Thank you so much. I don't know how to thank you."

"Just make sure she takes small bites. And pass up on the hotdogs when you can." He smiled at Lucy. "I'm glad you're all right."

Tiffani had believed all her life that doctors were only interested in themselves and how much money they could milk from someone in pain. Yet Rex Maxwell had just proved he was a doctor with a tender side and wasn't concerned about making money in a medical emergency. Her realization somehow made her feel unsure about a lot of things. Had doctors *really* been at the root of her family issues? Or could it have been something else? Thrusting the uneasy feeling aside, she forced herself to center on what really mattered here. She had some perfect material she could work with to pull off this job, get the promotion and finally escape Lou's ever-hovering presence in her life.

As they returned to their table Rex said, "Are you done with your meal?"

"Yeah."

"Then I'll pay." He picked his helmet up off a nearby chair and walked to the cash register.

She called after him, "While you do that I'm going to see if anyone got video of what happened."

He stiffened and said emphatically, "Please, don't." His response shocked her to the point of not arguing.

When they stepped out onto the sidewalk he glared at her. "What was that about?"

"That was good social media material. Stuff I couldn't

have planned." She couldn't keep her bubbling excitement to herself.

His face twisted in anger. "I didn't help that child to further your pointless campaign."

"I know that. But that was still great PR. I didn't start taking pictures until the girl was okay." She really hated to pass up this opportunity. "Oh, man, I need to have the mother sign an agreement to let me use Lucy's picture." Tiffani swiftly spun about, intending to go back inside.

He grabbed her phone as she turned.

"Hey, what're you doing?" To her horror she saw he was deleting the pictures.

"What happened in there is off the table."

Tiffani stared in frustration. "I have a job to do. The girl is fine. The public would love seeing you in action."

"Not going to happen. I didn't help the girl so you'd have something to put on social media," Rex spat out. Dropping her phone into her hand, he walked away.

By the time she reached her car, he was roaring away.

CHAPTER THREE

TIFFANI WAS STILL feeling the sting of Rex's reaction to her wanting to use the café emergency when she entered the assisted living home where her father lived. Rex's reaction had been so over the top. The girl was fine. The people in the café had seen him as a hero. They'd even applauded. She had too. So why couldn't she use it to their mutual advantage? He was the only one who seemed to have a problem with it.

The least he could do was understand she had a job to do. An important one. Maybe he didn't like the idea that he must be involved in the campaign but he had grudgingly agreed to help. Now he at least had some marginally professional-looking clothes and a hairstyle that both showed the real him yet made him look like a qualified surgeon. However, he'd skillfully manipulated those decisions to his advantage. Fighting with him at every turn was getting old. She sighed. It was like her entire life was built on difficult men. Her father, her ex and now Rex Maxwell.

Entering the extensive one-floor brick building, she walked down the wide hallway. Her father's room was close to the back. She wasn't sure if it had been his or the staff's choice to place him there. He could be difficult, but she loved him. She was old enough to remember well when he'd been in the car accident. Her mother had cried for days, driving them back and forth to the hospital to visit him. Her brother and sister, being younger than she, hadn't understood the tragedy as she did. It had been a long time before her father had come home. While he'd been gone, all kinds of people had come and gone at their house. First it had been friends, then workers, who'd made the doors bigger, rebuilt the bathroom and replaced the front stairs with a ramp.

Nothing had been the same again. Her father hadn't been home long before her mother had taken a job to help support them. That had left Tiffani alone to care for her father and her siblings. She'd learned to change her father's bandages, give him his medicines and assist him in any way he'd needed. He'd depended on her and she had been there for him.

Despite the loss of his legs he'd remained the commanding force in the family. Being with him, she'd heard daily how the doctors had taken his legs rather than save them. Had ruined his life. She had been taught to mistrust and second-guess anyone even remotely connected to the medical field. He was her father and she'd believed him without question.

She hadn't recognized it at the time but her father had begun growing more demanding and miserable. He drank regularly. Years had gone by before she'd discovered he'd taken too much of his prescription pain medicine too soon. He had been good with computers and electronics before the accident, but had made little effort to hold down a job afterward and had refused any vocational training. Their home life had deteriorated to the point that her mom had announced she was moving out, taking Tiffani's sister and brother with her.

Devastated, Tiffani had cried but couldn't go with

them and leave her father alone. He'd needed her. Who would take care of him?

It had taken work on her part when she had grown up, but she'd continued to visit him. She was the only one of her siblings who did and she saw him regularly. She even helped pay the difference between what it cost to live in the home and what he could afford.

Reaching the last room at the end of the hall, she knocked lightly on the door.

"Come in," came a gruff response.

To her amazement, her father sat in his wheelchair instead of being in bed. On more than one occasion she'd begged him to try the chair. Sadly, he had never made any real effort to use his prosthetic legs. His statement had always been, "If those damn doctors hadn't taken my legs, I wouldn't need those."

"Hello, Daddy." She pushed the door open. "How're you doing today? It's nice to see you out of bed."

"Hey, baby girl. Where have you been? I expected you thirty minutes ago."

As usual her father wasn't pleased she was there but was equally concerned about her being late.

"I was busy. I have a new client and a new campaign I'm working on." She hoped he wouldn't ask about her job because she didn't want to reveal her new PR project was a hospital and, worse, one of its doctors.

"I've been waiting for you to come so you can change the bandage on my hand."

He lifted it so she could see. There was white gauze wrapped around it, with tape holding it in place.

She looked at it with concern. "What happened?"

"I've been trying to use this wheelchair, like you wanted. Because of you, I have blisters," he accused.

As if she were the cause of the pain. Nothing was ever his fault.

But at least he was trying. "You know there're people here who can change a bandage for you."

"They don't do it right," he growled.

He'd become so dependent on her in those early days that he still demanded her care whenever he could get it. It wasn't unusual to have him call at any time of the day or night, begging her to come and do something for him. "Well, let me see what I can do."

"Baby girl. You're the only one that cares about me." His voice softened.

Tiffani sighed and kissed him on the forehead. "I love you, Dad." She gathered the supplies she needed from a drawer nearby, pulled a chair close to him and went to work. From years of practice she efficiently wrapped his hand. Seconds later she secured the bandage. "There you go. All done."

Her father raised his hand and waved it around. "It'll do."

That was all the praise she would get.

"You are having dinner with me," he said, wheeling backward one roll.

It was a demand, not a question.

In her most apologetic tone she informed him, "I've already had an early dinner so I'm not staying tonight."

"Why did you do that? You knew I'd want you to stay." The whiny tone had returned.

"I was with a client. We needed to talk over some things." This was a subject she did not need to go into detail on.

Yet he was watching her closely. "Like what?"

It was odd timing, but this was the most interest he'd ever shown in what she did for a living. Mostly she told him about what she was doing to distract him from complaining about something. Reluctantly she answered, "About what I needed him to do."

"Him? You're not back with that jerk you were seeing, are you?"

Her father had at least been concerned and supportive when she had told him about what Lou had done. For once the topic of conversation hadn't been her father. So why the interest this time? "I said he's my client."

"I hear something in your voice. What're you not telling me?" He wheeled closer, squinting at her suspiciously.

Her father had always been good at reading people. Even when he was drinking heavily he could catch a lie when she or one of her siblings told it.

"Nothing really." She put the bandaging supplies back in the drawer.

"Then why're you avoiding the question?"

She turned and looked directly at him. "Because I'm doing an image campaign for Metro Hospital."

Tiffani watched the shock, disbelief and then anger flow across his face. He flushed red. His hands went to the arms of the chair as if he were going to lift himself up. He barked, "You are what? That's where they took my legs. How could you do that to me?"

"Daddy, I'm not doing anything to you. All I'm doing is my job."

"But you're helping the hospital look all wonderful. Covering up what they really do to people there," he snarled.

"When your boss tells you to do something, you do it." She needed to calm him down or someone would come and check on them. She didn't want him to be thrown out of the center.

His voice rose with each word. "But you know what doctors do. You know how they treated me. You're helping the enemy."

Tiffani reached out to him. "I'm sorry, Daddy. I knew you wouldn't be happy but this campaign is important to my career."

He rolled away from her as much as the tiny space would allow. "I bet you're having to make doctors look and sound good. You know you can't believe what they say."

"I'm working with just one."

"Do I know him?" He gave her a pointed look.

It had been so long since her father's accident that most of the doctors he was familiar with were probably retired so she felt comfortable saying, "Dr. Rex Maxwell."

Her father pursed his mouth in thought before he blurted out, "Isn't that the name of the doctor involved in the malpractice suit that was all over the nightly news?"

Great, her father had been watching the news. She didn't look at him. "Yes. That's him."

"How could you, Tiffani? After what they did to me. My legs, my life." He waved his arms around, trying to express his furious frustration with her.

There was a knock on the door and one of the staff members stuck his head into the room. "Is everything all right down here?"

"Nothing's wrong except my daughter is a traitor," her father snapped.

The next day around mid-morning, having finished a case, Rex checked his phone messages. As he'd expected, there was a text from Tiffani, notifying him that she and the photographer were in the hospital. The text ended with her requesting he call the moment he was available. What if he ignored her? No. Tiffani would track him down. He wouldn't put it past her to show up in surgery. She'd not slowed down the last time she'd been after him.

The episode in the café the day before had not improved his opinion of her. The very idea of using pictures of that child's medical emergency to further Tiffani's agenda left him with a nasty taste in his mouth. He hadn't helped Lucy because it was a good PR move. He'd done what any dedicated doctor would do. His job was to save lives. Tiffani's opportunistic attitude appalled him.

Her comment about not caring for his profession struck him as odd. What did she have against doctors?

And still all this PR stuff painfully reminded him too much of his childhood. Dressing things up so they looked perfect and idealistic violated the promises he had made to himself. Straightforward honesty at all times was his motto. Yet here he was in a situation he wasn't completely comfortable with. The hospital provided exceptional care and he was who he was, an experienced physician. Neither of them needed some PR campaign to prove their worth. Still, he had agreed to participate in Tiffani's program.

Finally he texted back.

OK.

She replied.

We are in the conference room of the administrative suite.

Rex groaned and responded.

Only have thirty minutes till next case.

As he entered the conference room Tiffani made a beeline toward him. Today she wore pants emphasizing her curves and a flowing, ultra-feminine blousy shirt. To his disappointment, her hair was still worn up, this time tightly twisted behind her head. They might not agree ideologically but he had to admit he was intensely attracted to her and sought to know more about her. If nothing else, he wanted to see what she looked like with her hair down.

The meeting room had been transformed into a photography studio. The large table and chairs had been pushed against the walls. In their places stood a camera on a tripod, lights, a large backdrop that depicted the front of the hospital and a few other props. Besides Tiffani there was a man with a scruffy beard, wearing a vest, and two other people working at positioning props. Rex assumed they were the photographer's assistants.

"This is a bigger production than I anticipated," Rex murmured when Tiffani was at his side.

"We want to get pictures conveying confidence and trust," Tiffani informed him with an excited note in her voice.

The bearded man in the vest came over.

Tiffani took his arm, pulling him closer. "Dr. Maxwell, I'd like you to meet Luke Johnson, the photographer."

Rex offered his hand. "Make it Rex."

Luke nodded. "Nice to meet you. I'd like to get some shots of you dressed as you are before you change."

Rex looked through narrowed eyes at Tiffani. "Change?"

"Into one of the outfits we bought yesterday." Her expression was unyielding.

He did not have time for all this nonsense, but he'd given Nelson his word. The board would look dimly on it if he didn't cooperate as requested.

"Why don't you stand right here?" Luke suggested, indicating a spot in front of the backdrop.

"This is turning into more hoopla than I agreed to," Rex muttered, as he made his way to where Luke directed.

"I can assure you it's important," Tiffani replied.

Over the next few minutes Rex turned this way and that as instructed. Held his hands to his sides, crossed them over his chest and put them behind his back, all while smiling or not. Tiffani made comments here and there to Luke, occasionally placing her hand on his shoulder or looking into the camera before she gave Rex instructions to position himself a certain way.

Tiffani's obvious closeness to Luke deepened Rex's displeasure. Just how well *did* they know each other? Luke was a business associate, just like him, yet she paid him attention. She made it clear Rex was off limits. More perplexing and annoying was why he would care? He wasn't even sure he liked her.

It didn't take long until he'd had enough. Enough of having his picture taken. Enough of watching Tiffani so close to another man. Luke finally looked up from the camera said, "That was great. Now we're ready for the street clothes."

Perfect. There would be more of the same. Them using him as a mannequin while they huddled together and whispered.

Tiffani pointed to a screen in the back corner of the room. "You can change there."

"I don't have any more time for this. I'm expected in

surgery." Rex didn't even try to keep the irritation out of his voice.

Tiffani glanced at the clock on the wall. "It won't take long. According to the schedule Dr. Nelson provided, you have another twenty minutes."

Rex glared at her. "You should already have what you need."

"I need you in street clothes as well. It's better to do all the pictures at once than to have Luke come back later. When you're ready, we are. The clothes are behind the screen."

She was relentless. Like he cared if Luke was inconvenienced. It didn't matter to her that she was inconveniencing his surgical patients, let alone what he thought or wanted. Her job took precedence. Like yesterday with the choking girl.

More than that, he was unable to intimidate Tiffani. He wasn't used to that. His word was usually law. He wanted to assert his dominance over the irritating woman. At the moment that woman's and Luke's heads were almost touching as they studied the just-taken photos. Disgusted, Rex headed for the changing screen. The sooner he changed the sooner he would be done here.

He donned a sky blue shirt and khaki pants. To his great relief, there was no tie. There was a brown belt on a hanger, though. When he stepped from behind the screen Tiffani studied him before nodding, apparently satisfied.

"If you'll stand in front of the backdrop again," Luke said, looking through his camera on the tripod.

Rex took his spot once more. Luke clicked the button on the camera rapidly before asking Rex to turn another way. This entire ordeal was becoming more exasperating and frustrating by the minute. He was quickly reaching his limit on this silliness. Even so, he managed to give a pleasant smile on request.

When Luke stopped taking pictures and straightened, Rex's hopes rose. Maybe they were done with him. But a glance at Tiffani dashed his hopes. Her head was tilted and mouth drawn up in thought.

"Something's missing." A bright smile lit her face seconds later. "I know what it is. Anna," she said to one of Luke's assistants, "can you bring me that stethoscope?"

The girl picked it up from a chair and rushed to hand it to Tiffani.

Rex watched Tiffani approach. She was all business, viewing him as a figure she could manipulate this way and that. She didn't care about him. To her he was just the model for her damn PR crusade. For some reason that pricked his male pride. He didn't consider himself a vain man or expect every woman to find him appealing but he didn't appreciate Tiffani treating him as an object. The need to rattle her grew.

Reaching him, Tiffani held the stethoscope in both hands and raised it over his head. He didn't offer her help by bending so she could put it around his neck. She went up on her toes, causing her breasts to press against his chest. He burned where she made contact. Without any apparent reaction on her part, she slipped the tubing around his neck.

Watching her concentrated expression closely, he said soft enough that only she could hear, "My heart rate's up. How about yours?"

Her eyes widened and fixed on him. She stumbled. Rex put steadying hands on her waist. Her fingers gripped his shoulders. Hot seconds of awareness raced between them before Tiffani blinked and pushed away. His dented ego was bolstered by the red tint on her cheeks.

She kept backing away until Luke snapped, "Hey! Watch the camera."

Tiffani jerked around and sidestepped the equipment before going to the photographer's side. He immediately started taking pictures once more.

A minute later she said, "Anna, would you adjust the stethoscope so it doesn't hang quite so evenly? Pull it down a little on the right side."

Rex challenged Tiffani with a silent look, smug with the knowledge she was afraid to do it herself. He'd gotten to her. He smiled, emphasizing his unspoken invitation.

Tiffani averted her gaze.

Once Anna was out of the way, Luke resumed rapidly clicking, enthusiastically declaring, "That's it. The one we want."

Soon Tiffani announced, "That's all we have time for."

"I think we got what you wanted in that last batch, Tiffani." Luke started showing her the images.

Rex swiftly ducked behind the screen and dressed again. He left the "costume" piled beneath where he'd originally found it hanging. Tiffani didn't say anything as he left, but that was all right. He smiled as he strode down the hall. There was no doubt in his mind that she'd remember this photo shoot for a very long time.

CHAPTER FOUR

TWO DAYS HAD slipped by since Tiffani had last seen Rex. During that time she'd relived that instant between them at the photo shoot, when his breath had warmed against her skin. He'd had her so aware of the sexual tension between them she'd almost knocked over an expensive camera, trying to escape.

The man was outrageous. She must not let him get past her self-control. This campaign was too important. Rex was attractive but she could not afford to react to him like that. Nothing but pain followed that kind of arousing interest anyway. He was merely toying with her for his own amusement. Just as Lou had.

Yet in those few seconds she'd felt outrageously alive. Once again she had to admit that having a handsome man notice her bandaged her secret, still-raw wound.

Even with the heated thoughts running laps in her mind over the last few days, she'd managed to accomplish a great deal of work. So far, her plan was coming together nicely, in spite of Rex. Luke had promised to get pictures to her as soon as possible. The billboard company had three available and by the beginning of next week Rex would be on them, larger than life in front of a gorgeous shot of the hospital. She had also booked him on two morning shows. Now all she needed to do was continue to generate positive press and social media action, some of which would happen this weekend.

She sent Rex a text.

Can you meet me at nine in the morning at the hospital? I've arranged for us to visit a local clinic for a photo op.

Half an hour later her phone buzzed, notifying her of his answer.

Yes, but I pick the clinic.

What clinic? I need to let the photographer know.

Rex wrote back.

No cameras.

She didn't even try to change his mind. Any pictures she got she'd have to take on her phone. They would look less staged anyway. Perfect for what she had in mind.

The next morning, Tiffani arrived at the hospital at nine. As she walked across the parking lot toward the main entrance, a horn honked. An old orange truck was coming toward her. She hurried out of the way. At another short blast, she took a closer look. Rex was driving.

He pulled up beside her and leaned out the window. "Hey, good-looking, hop in and I'll give you a ride."

Rex thought she was attractive? Her stomach fluttered at the idea. She gave the truck a long disapproving look. In the movies, when a man used that old line he was usually driving a nice sports car. Grinning, he lifted one shoulder. "You're the one who told me to get something beside a motorcycle."

She quirked her mouth. "This isn't exactly what I had in mind."

"Don't be thinking bad thoughts about Bessie." He patted the dash. "She can get you where you need to go. Come on, have a little sense of adventure. Lighten up a little." He revved the engine. "See, she's raring to go."

Tiffani barked a laugh. "Okay. Just this once."

Rex leaned across the seat and pushed the passenger door open. She climbed in, grateful she'd worn jeans. "So Bessie is your spare vehicle?"

"Nope. I borrowed her from a buddy just for you. I knew from the way you turned up your nose the other day you wouldn't ride on my motorcycle."

She wouldn't have. After what had happened to her father, she had no intention of getting on one. Rubbing her hand over the old but clean seat, she said, "You're right about that. Where're we going?"

"To a clinic over in High Water," Rex replied, as he pulled out of the parking lot.

She couldn't keep astonishment out of her voice. "Really?"

"Yep."

High Water was an area of the city known for crime and poverty. Why had he picked there, of all places? For whatever reason, it would certainly make for good PR. She envisioned the headline: "Metropolitan Hospital's surgeon spends day off helping out in High Water." She couldn't go wrong with this material. Even so, she had to know. "Why there?"

"Because they need the help." His tone was flat and his eyes never left the road.

She studied him. He had both hands on the steering

wheel. They were capable and strong, which she was well aware of because they had been on her body. For some reason that thought sent a zip of heat through her. Firmly instructing herself not to go there, she asked, "What do you usually do on your days off?"

"Is that question work related or personal?" He gave her a brief glance.

"Maybe both. I just wanted to get to know you better." She really meant it.

"Mostly I work at the clinic."

"What?"

He changed lanes and headed toward an exit. "Don't sound so surprised. I work at the High Water Clinic. I helped start it, along with a couple of other doctors in town."

"You're kidding." She maneuvered in her seat so she could easily see his profile.

"You really don't have a very high opinion of me, do you? You've been reading what the newspapers have to say. Tiff, you do know you can't believe everything you read, right?" he asked in a singsong voice.

Tiff? Since when did he call her by a nickname? More important, how had she missed such a crucial PR point? "Nowhere in my research did it say anything about you being connected to that clinic."

He exited the interstate, stopped at a traffic light then turned to look at her. "Because it isn't public knowledge and I'd like it to stay that way."

"But this is perfect PR material. The morning shows will eat it up." Anticipation flowed through her. This campaign had a real chance of succeeding beyond her wildest dreams.

He grimaced. "Please, don't do that. These people are hard to win over. If you bring in news crews and they start asking all kinds of questions, it might take some of them years to trust the clinic again."

She tilted her head to the side. "Then why're you taking me?"

"I guess I wanted you to see the real me. That there's more to me than a pointless publicity project or the wild doctor who rides a motorcycle."

Why would that matter to him? A disturbed expression came over his face. Had he intended to say that out loud?

"Maybe, because you wanted us to go to a clinic and I was already coming here," he was quick to add. "All I ask is that you respect these people."

"Of course I will." What type of person did he think she was? Where had he gotten the impression she didn't care about people?

Silent minutes passed before Rex entered a neglected section of the city Tiffani had never visited. Many homes were abandoned and stores closed. Grass grew through the cracks and paper littered the gutters. Tiffani tried not to think about the fact that this was considered the highest drug and crime area of town, or the fact that it was frequently a main topic in the news. She should be feeling nervous but inexplicably Rex's presence made her feel safe, confident he could handle himself as well as take care of her.

A few blocks farther he pulled into what looked like an old grocery store parking lot. There were people mingling around the glass front. Paper covered the windows halfway up. On a cinder-block wall facing the parking lot were the words: High Water Clinic.

Rex climbed out of the truck and walked around to open the door for her.

Tiffani smiled gratefully and took his hand. It was

strong and sure. She was too aware of his touch. There was no place in her life for that reaction. He was a client, and moreover she had no intention of being hurt again. "You really do have nice manners. Thank you."

"Let's just say they were drilled into me." He smiled, easing the words. "Come on. They'll be waiting for us."

Tiffani couldn't decide if his disclosure was positive or negative. But it made her think about something besides her growing fascination with him.

He closed the door and remained close as they went to the front of the building, circling behind the people at the door, waiting to enter. Several of them spoke to Rex and he greeted them by name. Maybe he wasn't the self-centered doctor she'd originally judged him to be.

"The clinic generally doesn't open until nine thirty on Saturdays but there's almost always people lined up waiting before then," he informed her with a note of pride as he again held the door for her.

Inside was a large, dim room. Mismatched chairs lined the walls and a gray metal desk that had seen better days stood directly in front of the entrance. Behind it sat a heavy-set, middle-aged woman.

"Louise, you're looking ravishing this morning," Rex teased.

To Tiffani's amazement the older woman blushed.

"Don't you start with me, you charmer, you. Our day's going to be too busy for your nonsense."

"What's up?" Rex was all business now.

"We're short a nurse and doctor today. Dr. Bruster and Ronda both couldn't make it in today. Dr. Bishop is already seeing a patient and Amanda is assisting him."

Rex groaned. "I wasn't scheduled for today. I just came to show Tiffani around." He faced Tiffani with an apologetic expression. "I guess I need to get to work. I'm sorry about this."

He didn't sound put out or discouraged, just willing to do what was necessary. There was nothing of the prima donna she had expected to see. He continued, "I'll take you back to the hospital as soon as I can, but for now you're going to see how an all-volunteer clinic works. Smooth and efficiently." He chuckled, touching Tiffani's arm briefly.

Louise laughed. "Something like that."

There was nothing sexual about his touch but the awareness lingered long after he'd removed his hand. She was so distracted she didn't immediately realize he was speaking.

"Tiffani Romano, this is Louise Townsend, the glue that holds this place together."

"We both know that isn't true," Louise snorted. "Nice to meet you, Tiffani." She looked at Rex. "Now stop gabbing and get busy."

"Tiffani, you can wait here or there's a table in the back. Again, I'm sorry."

If she just sat around she wouldn't have any material to use. She wanted to see him in action. "Can I watch what you do?"

Rex's brows went up as if her request had astonished him. "You're sure you want to do that? You might be bored."

"More than I would be, waiting in the back room?" She gave him a direct look.

"Okay, as long as the patients are okay with it."

Louise waved a paper at Rex. "Here's your first patient."

Taking the paper, Rex gave it a once-over, opened the door to let people in and called, "Mrs. Guzman?"

A silver-haired Hispanic woman struggled through the door, a piece of cloth wrapped around her leg. Rex hurried to helped her. "Come with me. We'll see if we can get you fixed up."

Tiffani followed them to a hallway created by business office cubicles. Rex directed his patient to the first one on the right. After getting the okay from Mrs. Guzman, Tiffani followed them in. She wasn't sure she hadn't made a mistake by asking to watch Rex.

She was really stepping out of her comfort zone. She could count the number of times she'd seen a doctor on one hand—she avoided them unless there was no other choice—so this clinic was a foreign land in more than one way. What she *did* know was that doctors didn't know everything. She'd seen the devastation a wrong decision could make in a family's life. She wouldn't wish that on anyone.

Her plan had been to go to the clinic, take a few pictures of Rex tending to two or three patients, then leave. Never in her wildest dreams had she imagined she'd be in an exam room with him. At least she'd be getting a lot of material she could use. Maybe she could sneak a few pictures...

To Rex, Tiffani didn't look happy with the situation but she hadn't demanded to leave. For that she got positive points. At the clinic, she would get a close-up of his life as a physician. Guilt pricked him. He glanced behind him and spotted her standing in the far corner of the room. She really was a striking woman, but more than that she was intelligent, persuasive, most of the time too much, and today far too agreeable for his comfort. He might find he liked her more than he should if this continued.

Tiffani returned a weak smile in response to his reassuring one. He just hoped she wouldn't try to use the people here as part of her campaign. It had taken years for the clinic to build community trust. An overzealous PR person could mess that up. He should have gone to the clinic she'd planned on but he'd let his ego get the better of him.

"Mrs. Guzman, have a seat right here." He helped the woman to settle on the lone chair in the space they used as an exam room. "Tell me what the problem is."

"I burnt my leg."

"Let's remove that bandage and see what damage you've done," he said to Mrs. Guzman. "After I have a good look I'm going to need to make some notes."

"I can do that," Tiffani said.

Surprised, he almost forgot what he was about to say. "That would be helpful. Just write what I tell you. You can find a pad and pen in the top drawer of that box." He pointed to the red metal tool box the clinic used as a supply cart.

Tiffani nodded.

He turned back to his patient and removed the cloth. He heard Tiffani's slight intake of breath. It was an ugly burn. The skin was red and angry and a large blister had already developed. To Tiffani's credit, the slight sound was her only reaction.

"Mrs. Guzman, how did this happen?"

"I was up early this morning, canning tomatoes. I moved the hot pot to the sink and hit the counter and spilt scalding water down my leg." The woman shook her head. "I should have been more careful."

"Tiffani, please write down, 'Mrs. Guzman, second-degree burn to right shin.'" He trusted her to do as he asked and continued with his patient. "I'll need to clean this and then cover it in clean gauze. I'll get the supplies and be right back with you."

"I can do that if it'll help," Tiffani offered. "Tell me where to find the supplies."

He hadn't expected her to say that. "You sure?"

She nodded.

"Down the hall and around to the right you'll find a sink and cabinets. The liquid soap and bottles of saline will be sitting on the counter. There's a plastic tub under the sink you should bring too."

Tiffani stuffed the pad and pen into her back pocket and left.

"Mrs. Guzman, now tell me how you've been besides your leg," Rex said. Over the next few minutes he gave the woman a basic physical.

Tiffani soon returned, carrying the soap and bottle in the tub.

"Good. Put it all down here," Rex said, indicating the floor next to Mrs. Guzman's foot. No doubt soon Tiffani would be calling a cab so she could leave. Rex wouldn't blame her. He hadn't planned on her getting roped into being his nurse. "Now, Mrs. Guzman, just put your foot in here." He indicated the plastic pan. "I'm going to clean your leg." He patted her hand and she gave him a drawn smile. "Tiffani, please write on your notes, 'Cleaned with soap and saline.'"

She nodded then slipped out the door. Had she had enough?

He took plastic gloves out of the supply box and pulled them on then took out a small pile of four-by-four gauze pads. "Now, Mrs. Guzman, I'm going to pour the saline over your leg." Rex talked as he worked. Seconds later he was lightly applying soap with the pads, being careful not to damage the blisters. Done, he said, "We'll let that dry then I can I cover it."

"I could do that," Tiffani said from behind him.

She'd returned so quietly he hadn't realized she was there. He looked at her, trying to conceal his disbelief. "You sure?"

"Trust me, I've got it. I've had a lot of experience."

He could use the time to see more patients. "All right. Is that okay with you, Mrs. Guzman?" When the woman nodded, Rex stood, telling Tiffani, "The supplies are in the box. Third drawer down."

"Your next patient is waiting next door." Tiffani pointed as she moved toward the box.

She was full of surprises. She'd gone to get another patient while he worked? He admired her efficiency and forethought.

"Mrs. Guzman, I want you to keep this clean and wrapped until you come back next week and see the doctor. Tiffani will give you a couple of rolls of gauze to use. Can you do that for me?" He smiled at the woman.

She nodded.

"Good." He patted her shoulder. "Clean and dry is the ticket."

Again, the woman nodded. He left, with Tiffani chatting with Mrs. Guzman as she gathered the supplies she would need.

None of this scenario would he have ever imagined. Where had she learned to bandage to give her such absolute confidence she could handle Mrs. Guzman's injury? Rex was impressed. He couldn't think of another woman he knew who was outside the medical field but still would have stepped in to help.

His next patient was a two-year-old child whose mother looked fearful.

Rex went down on his heels and said to the mother, "Can you tell me what has been going on with Johnny?"

"He's crying a lot, pulling on his ears. Wants me to hold him all the time."

"Have him sit on the table and you hold him. I'm going to take a look in his ears."

Rex turned to his small patient, who now sat on the portable exam table. He hated the clinic's inexpensive furniture, but that wasn't the important thing. There was solid care here. He found the otoscope in the supply cart.

"Johnny, I need to look in your ears," Rex said, touching the boy's shoulder gently. After studying the ear's interior, he said quietly, "Now the other one." When done, he informed the mother, "He has an ear infection. He'll need an antibiotic. I can give you a few samples but you'll need to go to the pharmacy for more. Will you be able to do that?"

The mother nodded.

Just minutes later, Tiffani hovered by the entrance with paper and pen in hand. She was fast. *Good girl.*

Rex backed away until he stood close to Tiffani. There was that fresh floral scent he'd first smelled when she'd climbed into the truck. It was one he would remember long after he and Tiffani had parted ways.

"You need to write down—"

"I've already got it."

He stepped out into the hall. Tiffani followed him. "Thanks for the great help."

She seemed to glow under his praise, but then she appeared unsure, as if he might have said something wrong.

"It's better than being bored. Plus, I'm getting to see you in action." She continued to scribble.

"While I'm getting the medicine for Johnny, would you mind calling the next patient for me?"

"Already done. They're in the exam room next to this one."

He shook his head in disbelief and looked into her eyes. She was his type of woman. The kind willing to do what needed doing. "Thanks. You really have been great about this."

She shrugged and smiled.

"A PR woman on the way to being a nurse."

Her eyes flicked up to him. "That won't happen," she said, a hard note to her voice, and then returned to writing.

As he fetched the antibiotic samples, he pondered Tiffani's statement. She didn't seem to care much for his profession. There had been her look of uncertainty a moment ago. Yet she was doing a great job. Maybe her hang-up had to do with blood or needles? After giving the pill packs and instructions to Johnny's mother, he went to his next patient.

He saw Tiffani in the hall a few minutes later.

"I need to clean Mrs. Guzman's exam room," she said. "Tell me a few things about your last patient and I'll jot them down."

They worked seamlessly over the next hour, seeing five more patients. It took another couple of hours before there was no one else waiting. For what should have been a difficult clinic, Tiffani had managed to make it much smoother. At least for him. She walked down the hall toward him after dropping off some papers he'd asked her to take to Louise.

"I can run you back to the hospital now," he said.

"Don't we need to go over the patients' notes?"

A lock of her hair had come loose. He fingered the

glossy strand before he brushed it over her cheek and tucked it behind her ear. Tiffani stared at him. She looked vulnerable, approachable, all that PR businesswoman stuff suddenly missing. His gaze dropped to her mouth. What would she do if he tried to kiss her?

"Uh, you might not be able to read my writing." There was a hitch in her voice that let him know she hadn't been unaffected by his touch.

He grinned. "You do know you're talking to a doctor about penmanship."

"You do have a point."

"Let's go back here and make ourselves comfortable and see what you've got on those pages." He directed her toward the back of the building.

"My excuse is I had to write fast. What's yours?"

"I'll have you know I have better than average writing skills. Are you sure I don't need to be getting you back to the hospital, though?" He followed close behind her as they went down the makeshift hallway.

"No hurry," she said absentmindedly.

"What? No date on Saturday night?"

"No. Or any other night, for that matter." She looked stricken, as if she hadn't intended to make that confession out loud.

"I'd think someone as attractive as you would have a busy weekend planned." He directed her toward a folding table the staff used for breaks. "Would you like a soda? Some crackers? All out of a machine, I'm afraid, but the upside is I'm buying."

She put the small notebook and pen on the table. "Both, if you don't mind. My breakfast gave out hours ago."

Guilt niggled at him. She been stuck here, helping him. He would have to make this up to her. Rex dug in his pocket for some cash. "I'm sorry. I didn't intend to tie up your day. I owe you one."

"Well, I wasn't too happy at first but what kind of person would I be if I demanded to leave when you needed help so badly?"

"Now I really feel bad," he said over his shoulder as he headed to the vending machines.

"Don't. I've learned a lot more about you today than I ever would reading my research," she said across the room.

"I hope it was positive." He put his money in and made his choices.

"If you promise not to remind me I said this, I happen to be impressed. The wild, unconventional, push-the-limits doctor you'd have the world believe you are actually has a really big heart. And a nice bedside manner as well."

Why did he enjoy hearing those words so much, coming from her? Smiling, he turned around and put his hand over his heart in a mocking gesture. "Stop, you're making me blush."

Tiffani laughed. Big, full-bodied laughter that did something to his insides. He joined her. It felt good to joke with a woman. Few, if any, of the women he'd been in relationships with had enjoyed sharing witty banter. With them, the interaction had always been a prelude to sex.

It was nice to have a conversation with a woman who tested his mental sharpness. Getting to know Tiffani was turning into fun. Something he was sure she needed more of, and which he knew he could use too.

When their laughter subsided, she pointed her finger at him. "Now, don't you make me regret admitting that."

"I can't make any promises. Have a seat and we'll

look at those notes. If it's not too busy, maybe we can get out of here after I do some quick dictation."

Tiffani was glad to put her feet up, propping them on the chair next to her. The last time she'd done that much walking and standing on a hard floor had been during her college years when she'd worked at a chain store one summer. Despite her aching feet, the morning had been interesting and enlightening. She'd never considered how adaptable a doctor must be. Each case was different. Helping at the clinic had given her a whole new perspective on the medical profession, and Rex in particular.

She'd seen nothing of the uncaring, unresponsive person in Rex that her father had for decades accused doctors of being. Rex hadn't displayed an attitude with his patients. He'd acted as if he genuinely wanted to help them. His compassion and concern when interacting with his patients had seemed genuine. Even in Mrs. Guzman's case, which had been particularly unpleasant, he had tenderly cared for her leg with aplomb and concern.

There was none of the *I don't care* or *I'm more interested in getting you out of here* arrogance she'd believed. Had she taken her bitterness over what had happened to her father and, in turn, her family, too far by blaming *all* of the medical community?

Rex worked hard without complaint and never appeared irritated when there was just one more question. That she was impressed with him was an understatement. He was nothing like the doctor she had envisioned him to be. Just how fast Rex was growing on her pushed her outside the boundary of her comfort zone.

He put a couple of packs of crackers and drinks on the table then took a seat across from her. "May I see those notes?"

Tiffani pushed the notebook toward him. He flipped through the pages. "We don't keep extensive medical records here. Mostly notes we can pull out just to see what has happened before. Or how much medicine we've dispensed. Many of our patients have drug-dependency issues and we don't want to contribute to the problem. I'll get these dictated quickly."

"Does Louise type them up for you?"

He chuckled. "No. We have a lady who volunteers her time."

"Does anyone get paid who works here?" She opened her crackers.

Rex shook his head, his hair swinging around his head. "It's an all-volunteer clinic."

"Amazing."

"We're only open two Saturdays a month. I often think we'll not have enough workers and can't open but it hasn't happened yet. Almost happened today, but you saved the day." He gave her an approving smile before his attention was back on what she had written.

"That's me, Wonder Woman. Not." She made a self-deprecating sound.

"As far as I'm concerned, you were."

It was nice of him to think so. She had felt so humiliated after the fiasco with Lou that it was affirming to have a man appreciate her, even if it was just for stepping in to help.

Waiting for Rex to finish looking at her notes, she crossed her ankles, which were still propped up on the seat of the chair next to her. "This is an amazing place and obviously much needed."

"You can say that again," he replied, sounding almost absentminded, but then he gave her his full attention. "There are very few Saturdays when they're not waiting two and three deep to be seen. Today's cases were roughly normal but we have gotten some gunshot wounds and knife injuries. It was hard in the beginning to get people to come in, so many of them didn't trust us, but now we're flooded." His attention had gone back to her notes.

"I can well understand that," she remarked.

He looked at her. "Huh?"

"I grew up not trusting doctors." Her gaze met his as his mouth thinned.

"Why?"

She shrugged and took a cracker from its wrapper. "My father was injured in a motorcycle accident when I was in elementary school. He lost a leg almost at the hip and the other below the knee. He believes the doctors didn't do enough to save his legs because he didn't have adequate insurance. Even sued." She almost held her breath while waiting for Rex's reaction.

"He did, did he?" There was a bitter note in Rex's question.

"Consequently, I saw doctors as people to question. That you couldn't trust them. My father's accident broke up my family. He convinced my mother his opinion was truth. He didn't allow her to take my brother or sister or me to doctors. Thankfully we never had something serious happen. As the oldest I learned to be a pretty good home nurse. I had a lot of experience bandaging."

"I guess you did. I can't imagine getting through childhood without seeing a doctor, much less mistrusting them to the point you don't take your children to one."

When he said it out loud, it did sound rather awful. "I know it seems strange but when you know nothing different, you don't think much about it."

He picked up his drink and took a swallow. "So

when you said you didn't care for my profession, you weren't kidding."

"No."

"It must've been really difficult for you to accept this job once you learned what you were going to have to do for the hospital. And worse you would have to work with the doctor with a black mark by his name."

She fiddled with the cracker wrapper. "It wasn't difficult. Let's just say it was a concern. Especially since my father lost the malpractice suit."

"Why did you take the job, then?" He crossed his arms on the table, watching her with unnerving intensity.

"Because, unfortunately, making you and the hospital look good gives me a chance at a promotion I really want."

He clicked his tongue and set back. "Tough spot to be in."

"Not anymore. After seeing you in action today, I feel better about telling the world you're a great doctor."

Rex nodded. "I take that as high praise after what you've just told me." His hand grazed hers as he took the package from her and removed a cracker.

There was that tingle again she got every time he touched her. "Have you told your father what you're doing?"

"I have." She kept to herself the fact that she hadn't stayed more than a few minutes after he'd announced she'd betrayed him. But had she really?

"How did that go?"

"About as well as you'd expect." She tried to keep the sadness out of her voice.

"I'm sorry that hanging out with me has made things difficult between the two of you." Rex took a long swallow of his drink.

"That's not your fault. It's my job and my choice."

He pushed the chair back and stood. "Well, it seems we've both had wrong views of each other for the last few days."

Tiffani couldn't disagree with him about that.

Rex gathered up his half-full cracker wrapper and can, putting them in a garbage can. "I'd better get busy or you'll be stuck here all day. There's a small dictation room over there…" he indicated another cubicle "…where I'll be. It'll take me twenty or thirty minutes. We should be able to leave after that. Sorry you have to wait. You might find a magazine to read up front."

"I'll be fine. I'll see if Louise needs help with something after I finish my crackers and drink."

"I'll make this up to you, I promise."

She sat up and gave him an eager look. "Like letting me take pictures?"

He twisted up his face as if to refuse, yet compromised with, "I'll agree to one. Of my choice."

She sank back into her chair. "You aren't feeling *too* guilty, are you?"

"It's more that I need to respect these people." He headed off without another word.

After finishing her snack, Tiffani walked to the front of the clinic. Louise was busy filing papers.

She smiled at the older woman. "Can I help with something?"

"Put these in alphabetical order. Then file them here." Louise touched the filing cabinet behind her. "What's Rex doing?"

"He's busy working on reports."

"He's pretty special, isn't he?" the old woman asked.

Yes, he is. Too much so for Tiffani's comfort.

CHAPTER FIVE

REX FOUND TIFFANI elbow deep in papers after he'd completed his dictation. "You didn't have enough to do this morning so now you're doing paperwork?"

She glanced at him. "I'll be finished here in a sec."

"We could use her around here all the time," Louise said.

He doubted that would happen. Tiffani had only been there that day because she hadn't known what she'd been getting into. He said to Louise, "I'm going to run Tiffani back to her car and get some lunch. You want me to bring you anything?"

"I'm good. I've eaten lunch."

A few minutes later Tiffani said, "I'm ready. See you later, Louise."

"Thanks for the help, honey," the woman called as they went out the door.

"I'll see you in an hour," Rex said. "You sure made an impression on Louise."

"I can usually get along with most people. You're the only one who's had a problem with me in some time."

Rex stopped and she did too. He looked at her as they stood in the parking lot. "Is that so? What issue did the last one have?"

"One I don't want to talk about. You know, I haven't

gotten that picture you promised. How about you under the clinic sign?" She pointed to the one on the wall above his head.

When he didn't immediately agree she narrowed her eyes and said, "You promised."

"Okay." He turned his back to the wall and faced her.

"I need a smile." She gave him an example.

"I am smiling."

She grinned. "That's more of a grimace."

"Will this do?" He gave her his best pleasant smile.

"I guess so, but I would've much preferred one like you gave Johnny this morning after you checked his ears."

She'd been watching that closely?

"I only have one of those a day to give away." He opened the truck door for her. As she was getting in she looked back at him, their faces almost at the same level.

"That's a shame," she said softly. "It's such a nice one."

A warmth he wasn't familiar with filled his chest. What *would* she do if he kissed her? For some reason, that thought kept coming to mind. He wasn't interested in teasing her anymore. He wanted to really kiss her. Hold her against him. Hear her sigh with pleasure. See if her lips tasted as soft and delicious as they looked.

Before he could act on that desire, she gave the door a tug to close it. He stepped out of the way. The moment was lost. He would regret that missed opportunity.

As he drove away he said, "I'm going to get a drive-through burger. You want one before I take you back to your car?"

"No, thanks. I've got to go home and cook a meal for my father so I'm good."

Rex certainly wasn't going to get an invite to that,

knowing how her father felt about doctors. Why would he even be interested in going? He wasn't a meet-the-parents type of guy. He'd just go to one of the clubs and catch some good jazz music. After all, he and Tiffani were in a business relationship. Nothing more.

On the way to the hospital they chatted about their morning. Soon he was pulling up behind her car. He hopped out and went around to open her door.

"You do know that I'm capable of doing that for myself, don't you?"

"It's not about you being capable but about me being polite." Watching her closely, he held the door wide but stood so she couldn't easily get around him.

"Is something wrong?" Her gaze met his.

"I was just wondering if I tried to kiss you, would you let me?"

He didn't wait for an answer. His lips found hers. They were just as soft and inviting as he'd imagined. When she didn't move he placed his hands on her waist and pulled her to him. Tiffani felt so good. She didn't push away, she just accepted. But he wanted her to reciprocate. He moved his mouth over hers in hungry invitation. She returned his kiss. Rewarded him with that sigh he'd wished for.

Seconds later she pushed him away, her look having turned cold and distant. "Please, don't do that again."

He didn't know if he could promise her that. "Why not?"

"I don't like to be played with."

Why would she think he was doing that? "Who said I was?"

"Like you really want to have a relationship with me. Up until today we barely tolerated each other."

"Whoa, it was just a simple kiss, not a shot fired

across the bows of your boat or a marriage proposal."
He backed away. "I didn't mean to insult you."

Her glare burned into him. "You didn't insult me.
I just came out of a bad relationship and don't wish to
repeat it."

"So you're saying that by kissing me you almost
started another bad relationship?"

Tiffani moved farther away from him. "Right now,
I need to concentrate on my job. Our interactions have
to remain professional."

"Based on that kiss, which was far too short, that
might not be possible." He took a step toward her.

"Then you'd better figure out how to make it so.
Thanks for an informative day. I'll be in touch." With
those words, she presented him with her back and hurried to her car.

"Tiff." He waited until she looked at him. "It might
be you who has to work at that."

Looking stricken, she climbed into the car.

What had just happened? He'd given a girl he was
attracted to a simple kiss and she'd made it plain she
wasn't interested. But there had been a second there
when she'd returned his kiss that proved she wasn't immune to him. Tiffani was just scared. But was she scared
of him or herself?

When Tiffani started her car, he came out of the daze
she'd left him in. He slammed the passenger door closed
and went around to the driver's side. Getting in, he put
the truck into gear and drove off.

He wasn't afraid to go after what he wanted.

Tiffani's hands shook on the wheel of the car as she left
the parking lot. Rex had kissed her. She'd liked it. Better than liked it. But it must *not* happen again. It was

wrong on a professional level. A personal one too. She couldn't handle someone with such a large personality after what had happened with Lou. She wasn't prepared for humiliation again. Nothing more than a fling could happen between Rex and herself anyway. They were too different. She refused to let herself be played with again. Once was more than enough.

She'd made the right decision to push Rex away. Yet a part of her wished she hadn't. She wanted him to kiss her again. Wanted the chance to run her hands through his mess of hair. His lips hadn't demanded; instead, he'd teased and tested as if telling her he could be patient. That he would wait for her until she was ready, until she could trust him. When she had given in and kissed him back, she'd found pleasure she hadn't known existed.

Being kissed wasn't new to her but even the almost chaste one from Rex left all the others lacking. But she was going to have to forget about it and put all her energy into earning that promotion. If she did get it she'd be moving anyway. There were too many ways that Rex Maxwell was wrong for her.

At least she had no reason to interact with him again for a few days. That would leave her time to get her mind going in the right direction. She'd make sure she was back in professional mode before she saw him again.

On Monday morning, she opened her emails to find that Luke had sent over the proofs of the pictures of Rex for the billboards. She searched through them. The camera had captured Rex's masculine attractiveness. When she'd been putting the stethoscope around Rex's neck Luke had continued taking pictures. He had caught that moment Rex had whispered to her. She hardly recognized herself. The wonder on her face. Even now warmth washed through her.

Tiffani swallowed and clicked the picture off the screen.

She'd trust Luke's opinion on the best picture to use for the billboards. By the weekend Rex's picture would be up around the city. She pulled out her phone and searched for the picture she had taken at the clinic. In a few minutes, she would have that out on social media. Hopefully it would generate some positive buzz.

Later that day, she reported to her boss about her progress with the campaign. He seemed pleased. Tiffani returned to her desk and picked up her phone. She'd been putting off the necessary phone call all day. Had Rex been thinking about her as much as she'd thought about him? She didn't need to go in that direction. There was business to attend to and her objective focus was required.

She punched in Rex's number. With any luck he wouldn't answer and she could just leave a message. On the third ring disappointment set in.

"Rex," was barked in her ear halfway through the fourth ring.

Her heart jumped in panic at the sound of his voice. "It's Tiffani."

"Hey, Tiff. Give me a second. I'm right in the middle of something." He seemed distracted.

"I'll call back." There was no response. Instead, she listened as he spoke to someone else. A minute later he said, "Sorry about that. I'm just coming out of surgery."

"This can wait."

"No, I can talk now. How've you been?" His voice relaxed on the last three words.

"I'm fine."

"I've missed seeing you." His voice was soft and deep.

He was flirting with her. If he kept that up it would be difficult to resist him. "I wanted to let you know I have an interview set up for you on WMEP *This Is Memphis* on Thursday morning."

"I may have surgery scheduled then."

The Rex she could handle was back.

"I can't rearrange my schedule," he continued. "My patients come first. What is it anyway?"

It was progress that he even asked that. "It's the most popular local morning show."

"I haven't seen it. I'm usually in the OR before those come on."

"Rex, this is an important interview. We'll work around your schedule. I need you to do this one," she pleaded.

"And what's in it for me?"

She didn't miss the suggestiveness in his tone. "Making the hospital look good."

"Come on, Tiff. You can do better than that," he teased, but there was a hopeful note in there as well.

Every time he called her Tiff she quivered. "I've already asked Dr. Nelson if we can set up in one of the consult rooms near the OR. You can do the interview in your scrubs. It'll look more authentic anyway. When the interview is over you can go straight back to surgery. How does that sound?"

"Like you're being all business. I'd still rather not do it. Again, what's in it for me?"

"It'd make me happy." Tiffani kept her voice even.

"That's better but still not good enough."

There was the faint sound of his name being called before he said, "I've got to go. I'm looking forward to seeing you Thursday."

Even over the phone Rex had her thinking of things better left alone. Thursday couldn't come soon enough.

It was around mid-morning when Rex entered the small consult room just steps from the surgery suite. Once again the table and chairs had been moved against the wall. This time there was a great deal more equipment than there had been for the photo shoot. Two large light stands, glowing brightly, faced two tall chairs situated close together, almost facing each other. Heavy-duty electrical cables ran along the floor. Two men stood behind two different cameras on tripods.

He'd walked into another world. A world he didn't understand and where he had no control. The urge to leave grabbed him.

Tiffani wore an expensive suit with matching shoes that made her look as edgy as she acted while she conversed with a blonde woman he recognized from billboards around town. As the women talked, they kept referring to a piece of paper. He didn't turn on the TV or often listen to the talk stations so he had no idea if the woman had given the malpractice case a lot of air time.

Tiffani glanced his way, said something to the woman and came to meet him. "Hey, there. Glad you're here." Her smile was hesitant.

Had she been nervous about seeing him? He liked that idea. If he had her uncertain then he had a chance. She would be more open to getting to know him better. He hadn't had to chase a woman since high school. Doing it now was both exciting and daunting.

"I've missed you."

"Rex!"

He grinned. "Well, it's true." Glancing around, he noted, "There sure is a lot of stuff here just for a short interview." Weren't these the same people who'd had nothing kind to say about the hospital weeks ago? "I don't have much time so can we get started?"

"They've almost finished setting up." She moved toward the set chairs on the set and he followed. "All I want you to do is answer questions honestly and positively. Remember this is about improving the hospital image."

"I always answer honestly."

She looked at him. "Don't forget the positive part."

The blonde woman joined them. She wore makeup so heavy she appeared cartoonish. Extending her hand, she announced, "I'm Maggie Martin. You must be Dr. Maxwell."

"Please, call me Rex." He took her hand. It held no warmth.

Maggie's smile was syrupy. "It's nice to finally meet you."

Rex nodded acknowledgment then gave Tiffani a winsome smile.

"We'll be ready in just a minute," Maggie said as she hurried away. Over her shoulder she added, "I'm glad you're wearing your scrubs. I like a touch of authenticity."

"I'm in scrubs because I am an authentic surgeon," he muttered through gritted teeth, watching her go.

Tiffani touched his arm lightly. "Be nice. Also, would you mind taking off your head cover? And you'll need to see the makeup person."

This was getting worse every second. "Why do I need makeup?"

"Please, Rex. It won't be much. This is too important. Please, just go along with it," Tiffani begged.

He leaned in close so that only she could hear him. "You know, I like the sound of my name on your lips."

Her blush was his reward. "Stop," she hissed. "Come on over here."

Rex wasn't sure the hospital's image was worth this aggravation as Tiffani led him to a young woman. "She'll do your makeup and brush your hair."

Rex narrowed his eyes and tightened his lips to let her see his disgust before she hurried off. Five minutes later the woman pronounced him ready for the camera and directed him to the chair on the right. He took the seat. One of the assistants hurried over and attached a tiny microphone to the V of his top and clipped the power pack to the waistband of his pants in the back.

Maggie joined him, settling in the other chair. Tiffani stationed herself beside one of the cameramen in front of a monitor.

"Rex, I'll be introducing you then we'll just talk. Easy-peasy," Maggie quipped.

Something warned him not to believe it would be that simple. This couldn't be over soon enough.

"Okay, here we go," Maggie said.

Rex straightened, eyeing Tiffani. She gave him a reassuring smile. He returned a less enthusiastic one. Because he had nothing to hide he wasn't nervous, but it was nice to have Tiff on his side.

"Good morning, Memphis," Maggie announced with professional enthusiasm. "Today we have a very special treat for you. We're coming to you live from Metropolitan Hospital. We're going to highlight the hospital and share a little bit about what happens in the daily life of the staff here. A staff made up of many dedicated and special people. This morning we're talking with Dr. Rex

Maxwell, a surgeon here at Metro." Maggie turned toward him and beamed. "Welcome, Dr. Maxwell."

"Good morning." He answered with all the pleasantness he could muster.

"I'd like to start off by asking you to tell us what a usual day would be like for you."

He glanced at Tiffani. Her expectant smile reminded him how important this interview was to her. He'd agreed to do this, so to please her he would play the game and play it well.

"I'm a general surgeon. Most of my cases are people who come through the ER. My typical day starts at five thirty in the morning and I'm at the hospital by six. I do paperwork and see patients until seven, when my surgery schedule starts. After that I see patients in ICU or on the floor." How he could have said more and told less, he didn't know.

Maggie nodded, wearing a thoughtful expression. "Wow, that sounds like a busy day."

He'd leaned forward a little, tilted his head. "Some days more so than others." A covert glance at Tiffani made him think she was pleased with his efforts.

Meanwhile Maggie gave him a practiced smile. "I understand that recently you and the hospital were involved in a malpractice suit. Would you care to comment on that?"

There it was. What his gut had told him was coming. His gaze found Tiffani. She wasn't moving a muscle and her expression implored him to give a positive answer. Was she afraid he was going to lose his temper? Taking a page from Tiffani's playbook, he went on the offensive.

Leaning closer to Maggie as if he were going to tell her a secret, he said, "I can't say much but I'll tell you this. I use every skill I have to care for and save lives.

Every time I, or my fellow surgeons, enter the OR our priority is saving patients' lives. Our livelihoods are the last thing on our minds when we're operating. This hospital puts its patients first in every case. Sometimes we simply can't win the war between life and death, but we do everything within our knowledge and with our experienced skills to fight the battles."

Maggie blinked, as if she needed a moment to regroup, then asked, "So you're telling me there was nothing to the malpractice suit?"

Rex sat back and clasped his hands in his lap. "When your loved one dies, it's only natural to seek a source of blame."

"Does that mean you're not guilty?" Maggie's look bored into him.

Rex squared his shoulders. He wasn't going to rehash old news for anyone. "No one likes being accused of doing something they didn't do. How many stories have you had to retract? Or weather forecasts have you issued that turned out to be wrong? Should you be fired for acts of God?"

Maggie's head jerked back as if she was astonished. "I guess we've all faced that at one time or another."

"That's true. But most people don't have to live with the accusation they caused someone's death or the fear they might lose their job because of something completely out of their control." Rex held her gaze with confident humility.

Maggie's eyes softened and her voice became sympathetic. "I imagine you do have some days when it's hard to go to sleep."

He smiled. "Yes, I've had more than a few. But I love my job and find being a doctor rewarding." Sneaking another look at Tiffani, he was relieved to see she no longer appeared worried.

Maggie's fake smile turned genuine. "Tell us why you wanted to become a doctor."

"Well, Maggie, I worked at a local nursing home when I was a teenager. I needed a job and wanted to do something where I could make a difference."

She nodded and leaned toward him. "So tell me, what does a surgeon do in his off time?"

"I don't know, what does a popular newscaster like to do?" He winked at her.

Maggie giggled. "You sure there's nothing you want to tell?"

He gave her his best grin, hoping it looked sincere. "It isn't an adventure if you know the destination." He then relaxed against the back of his chair.

"Before you get back to work, I'd like to know if you're participating in the Walk with a Doc event sponsored by the hospital and this station this weekend?"

Rex looked at Tiffani. She put up her hands in a praying manner and nodded her head.

"I wouldn't miss it." He tried to sound eager.

Maggie looked at the camera. "So everybody come out and join Dr. Maxwell and I this Saturday for a chance to Walk with a Doc in Tom Lee Park. As well as the walk, there will be qualified medical professionals providing free health checks." She turned back to him. "Dr. Maxwell, thanks so much for being here with us today."

Rex nodded, relieved it was over, and as the cameras cut out, the assistant quickly came over and removed his microphone. Tiffani's smile was wide, happy. It was nice to have her pleased with him. To have earned her genuine pleasure.

* * *

Tiffani couldn't believe her eyes or ears. Rex had actually had Maggie flirting with him. He'd used his charm to get around her probing questions and had come out the winner. The hospital had as well. The interview could have been a train wreck but he'd turned it into a PR triumph.

She watched as he stood, speaking to Maggie one more time, then came over to her. She met him halfway. Without thinking, she threw her arms around his neck and hugged him. "You were great!"

His arms encircled her, pulling her against the hard wall of his body. "Thanks. I'll take a rain-check on your enthusiastic expression of gratitude because I have to go. They're waiting for me in the OR."

Tiffani quickly released him, feeling heat flushing her face.

He whispered, for her ears only, "Don't ask me to do that again."

"But I had another in the works for next—"

"I won't do it. I'm not explaining my actions. Especially when I wasn't guilty of anything." He walked away and out of the room.

Was he going to fight her on every front? He'd done an excellent job and now he wanted to quit. Today's interview was the type that changed people's minds. It helped them to see him as a person, a dedicated doctor, significant. Was there something more than the malpractice suit eating at him?

She would be seeing him on Saturday for the Walk with a Doc event. At least he'd committed to it and she wouldn't have to blackmail him into going. Maybe while they were there she could work on convincing him he needed to do more interviews. He'd been a natural on-camera, and discussions like those were the perfect outlet for her PR campaign.

Really, though, with his charm, anything that involved a woman was his forum. Maggie wasn't the only one captivated by Rex. No matter how Tiffani tried to deny it, she too was quickly falling under his spell.

CHAPTER SIX

RINGING WOKE TIFFANI early on Friday morning. She rolled over, grabbed her cellphone and glanced at the number. Rex. Her heart skipped. Thoughts of him had been circling in her head all night and none had to do with the campaign. Why was he calling now? Had something happened?

"Hello."

"Hey, there, sleepyhead." He sounded far too cheerful. "If you don't want me to arrive on my bike tomorrow I'm going to need you to come by and pick me up. My buddy needs his truck."

By the tone of his voice he was enjoying the idea of making her his chauffeur for the day. Regardless, she didn't want him arriving on his bike for the Walk with a Doc event. She didn't want any opportunity for negative publicity about Rex to present itself, not when the campaign was going so well after his interview. There had been a huge amount of positive feedback on social media regarding the "cute doctor." She didn't need any damaging press right now.

"What's your address? I'll be around to get you about seven thirty tomorrow morning."

"Great, then I'll see you bright and early." Rex gave her an address that she recognized as being in the historical district, then said goodbye, leaving her alone with her thoughts about him.

On Saturday morning, Tiffani was up and out of bed earlier than normal. For reasons she refused to examine, she took longer than usual deciding what to wear, refusing for a second time to think about why she felt a deep-seated need to look nice for Rex. She decided to forgo the PR attire in an effort to appear more feminine and casual. After careful consideration she chose a short-sleeved, red button-down shirt and black skinny jeans. As a final touch, she pulled her hair up into a loose ballerina bun.

Rex's neighborhood had recently gone through rejuvenation. Young families and professionals were moving back. Trendy restaurants and jazz bars were in abundance. The famous Beale Street was only a few blocks away. If she could afford it, the area would be a place she would enjoy living.

Tiffani pulled up in front of the address Rex had given. It was a red brick building with the type of tall windows she'd always found especially appealing.

She pulled to the curb and texted him.

I'm here.

In less than a minute he came out of a dark wooden door and headed toward her. His hair was pushed away from his face and held by a ball cap worn backward. The T-shirt he wore fit him well enough to reveal his muscular chest. She acknowledged to herself, with a bit of guilt, that his jeans and tennis shoes suited him better than the "business" clothes she'd coaxed him into wearing for the photos. However, she had no choice but to present him as a polished, competent professional on the billboards.

His smile was broad as his eyes met hers through the windshield. It was refreshing to have someone glad to see her. Her father was only happy to see her when he wanted something and Lou had never exhibited such a look of joy when he'd seen her.

"Mornin', Tiff," Rex said as he climbed in. "Man, I forgot about how small your car is." He worked to get his long legs inside. "Will you help me out if I need it?"

She giggled. "That would be a good clip for the media. Me bent over your lap."

His look caught hers. "Sounds interesting to me."

She felt the rush of heat from head to toe.

Although he'd turned her remark into a naughty image, he might really need her assistance in getting out. His knees pressed against the dashboard even with the passenger seat as far back as it would go.

Rex remarked, "If I hang out with you much longer, you're either going to have to get on my bike or buy a larger car."

Was he thinking about them spending more time together? She had been. Despite his attitude about the campaign, she'd discovered she liked him. Liked how he had challenged her in the past few days to step out of her secure world.

She mustn't let herself think about such things. If, no, *when,* she got the promotion, she was moving out of town. She certainly didn't need a long-distance relationship that would no doubt end in another ugly breakup. She had sworn to herself she wouldn't go through that hell again.

It had rained near daybreak and the early morning streets were still damp. There were no clouds in the sky now, but in their area of the south it wasn't uncommon to get storms late in the afternoon.

Finding a parking spot near Tom Lee Park, she pulled in. Rex did have some difficulty getting out but, thankfully, he didn't request her help. They walked toward the staging area near the entrance of the park with the wide flowing Mississippi River on one side. She would miss it when she left. Tiffani glanced at Rex. He might be something else she'd miss as well.

Tents were set up in a grassy area with tables and chairs under them. People mingled while others worked to prepare for the event. As she and Rex moved toward the starting/finishing line, marked by a high arch of balloons, she overheard one woman say to another, "Isn't that the doctor on the billboard?"

"What're they talking about? Have the billboards already gone up?" Rex immediately demanded.

Tiffani stopped. He did too. She turned and pointed toward a billboard just barely visible in the distance on which Rex was bigger than life, standing in front of the hospital in his dress shirt, stethoscope around his neck, arms crossed over his chest and smiling with self-assurance. Everything about the picture generated an impression of you-can-have-confidence-in-me.

"I'm sure they're talking about that one, but there are others around town."

Rex groaned as if in pain. "The people I work with are already making fun of me about the interview. This isn't going to help things. How many are there?"

"Three, and I hope to put up a couple more. I wanted them in the most prominent places so I'm having to wait until space becomes available."

"You're killing me, woman." He started walking again.

Grinning, Tiffani caught up. "I told you I planned to do billboards as soon as possible."

"Yeah, but I didn't really think it through." He looked disgusted. "I'm so…large."

"But at least you're handsome." Tiffani realized too late what she'd said.

Rex smirked his pleasure. "So you think I'm handsome?"

"You're not going to pull me into that conversation." She walked faster.

He called after her, "You can't run and hide. I heard you."

She was glad when they reached the starting area. The WMEP crew was already setting up.

If she could manage it, Tiffani planned to have Rex do another quick interview with Maggie. Tiffani was certain it wouldn't be a problem after Maggie's reaction to him on Thursday. He'd charmed her without a doubt, but Tiffani knew convincing him to do another interview would be difficult.

"Hey," she said, as if on impulse, "I know you don't like all this limelight but I really do appreciate you working with me. I reported how things are going to Dr. Nelson yesterday. He seemed pleased and implied that the board would be as well."

"I'm glad someone's happy," Rex grumbled.

"Today would be another big boost if you'll just be agreeable. Would you do a short interview with Maggie about the event today?"

"I'm always agreeable," he said in a snide tone.

She gave him a dubious look and put her hands together in a praying manner. "Will you, please?"

He sighed deeply, giving her an uncertain look. Just

when she expected him to refuse, he said, "I'll do it if you really think it's necessary."

"I do. I'll go see if I can find Maggie." Tiffani hurried off with a smile on her face.

Rex watched Tiffani walk off in the direction of the TV van. She had a sweet little tush. One he wanted to cup and pull against him. Yet she behaved as if she had her elbows locked to keep him at arm's length. All she seemed to think about was her campaign. He consoled himself that at least they would have some personal time during the walk.

He liked these types of events, even though he didn't often get to participate in them. Most of his time was tied up at the hospital or the clinic. This morning was pleasant and the crowd was animated, clearly eager to have a good time, so he was going to make the most of it.

"Rex."

He looked in the direction of the call. Tiffani was waving at him. He strolled over to her.

"Maggie said she'd love to talk to you."

At least one woman was interested in him, just not the right one. "If I must."

Tiffani gave his arm a light slap. "Be nice. You were great last time."

Before he could respond, Maggie and a cameraman descended on them. "Hello, Rex. It's so nice to see you again."

Tiffani's eyes narrowed but a smile remained on her face.

"Maggie, it's a pleasure to see you too." He used his most pleasant voice, thankful for his perfect manners.

Over the next few minutes she asked him about why he was participating in the Walk with a Doc event and about what he did to remain healthy. A couple of times she rested her hand on his arm. The first time he happened to glance at Tiffani and found her lips pursed as she watched them intently. When it occurred again he made a point of looking at Tiffani. Her brows had narrowed and she took a step forward before she stopped.

Did she not like Maggie touching him?

Maggie finished the interview and the camera was off when she gripped his forearm and cooed, "Call me sometime. You can reach me at the station."

A second later Tiffani said, "Rex, we'd better go. It's about time to line up."

As if on cue, an announcement that the walk was beginning could be heard loud and clear.

Rex said in his best syrupy voice, adding a smile, "Thanks, Maggie. Bye." He called after Tiffani, who was stalking away, "Hey, what's the hurry?"

She stopped and looked at him. "What?"

"Why the rush? We have time."

"I was afraid that if I didn't get away from you two I might go into a diabetic coma with all that sugar piling up," she answered in a sarcastic tone.

A slow grin came to his lips. "I don't think I've ever felt more flattered."

Perplexed, she demanded, "What're you talking about?"

"You're jealous." He couldn't stop his huge self-satisfied smile.

"I am not!" she huffed, then hurried off.

"I thought you wanted me to be nice to her." Rex continued after her.

She stopped and glared at him. "I wanted you to look like a professional that people could trust, not a man looking for a date."

Rex burst out laughing. "I was carrying on a conversation. She was the one doing all the touching."

"And from what I could tell, you were eating it up." Tiffani huffed a second time and disappeared into the crowd.

Rex found her waiting near the starting line. He grinned and she looked away. Here he was, thinking he wasn't getting through to her and, lo and behold, she was jealous. That was a giant step in his favor.

The crowd gathered around them. As they did so, Tiffani took pictures of them and several of Rex.

He asked, "What're you doing?"

"I'm getting some shots to put up on social media, the hospital newsletter and website. They might not be as engaging as Maggie's interview but they'll be more about the hospital and less about flirting." She raised her chin. "Plus, these you can't forbid me to use."

His nose almost touched hers. "I bet I can."

She lifted her head haughtily. "But I'm not going to listen."

A representative of the hospital, using a microphone, demanded their attention. He welcomed everyone then asked all the doctors to raise their hands. Rex put his up. The crowd around them cheered. The man then said a few more words about the importance of wellness before he called out, "Ready. One, two, three, walk!"

The mass of bodies surged around Rex and Tiffani. For a second he feared he might lose her and grabbed her hand. Her head jerked around, her look rebellious as she tried to free her hand. He held tight. "I don't want to lose you."

With a trace of hesitancy in her eyes she stopped resisting.

They followed the route designated by arrows down

the path along the river. He'd reviewed a map before-hand and knew they were following a large circular path through the park. Others strolled, deep in private conver-sation, around them. When the crowd thinned, Tiffani pulled her hand free. He let her go without argument, even though he missed the soft feel of her flesh next to his. He set his pace to hers.

They hadn't gone far when a girl of about twelve came up beside him, pointing to the billboard, which was now easier to see. "That's you up there on that sign, isn't it?"

Tiffani took a picture of them.

He wasn't going to enjoy having the billboards around town. What had he been thinking to agree to it all? "Yes, that's me."

"You're famous?"

Tiffani made a choking noise.

He glared at her then looked at the girl again. "No, I'm not famous."

The girl seemed satisfied and ran off to join a group ahead of them.

Through clenched teeth he warned, "Tiff, don't you dare say anything."

Her giggles filled the air around them, eventually fading away as they continued to walk.

The ensuing silence between them was comfortable.

Minutes later she said, as if talking more to herself than him, "I love this city. I'll miss it when I leave."

His chest tightened. "You're leaving?"

"I hope so. If I get that promotion then I'll move to the home office."

He looked at the railed bridge ahead across the river. "Where's that?"

"Louisville, Kentucky."

He whistled low. "That's a long way away from here."

"It is. It'll be a big change but a good one." She sounded more resigned than excited.

Rex didn't want to scrutinize the uneasy feeling in his stomach. "How soon is this supposed to happen?"

"If this campaign goes well, I hope soon." She gave him a serious look then took pictures of people ahead of them.

The thought of her leaving had him suddenly thinking of ways to sabotage the campaign. But why was he overreacting? They hadn't even been on a date. A fact he decided to remedy right then. "Do you like barbecue?"

She gave him a look of disbelief. "Yeah. How can you live in Memphis and not like barbecue?"

"Wet or dry?" he asked as they made the turn and headed back the way they had come.

"Both, but dry is usually my pick." She clicked a few more pictures.

"Mine too. How about we go for lunch when we're done here? I know a great place that serves a special dry rub."

Her step faltered for a second. Rex grabbed her arm to steady her. When she was surefooted again he released her.

"I don't know if that's such a good idea," she finally said.

"Why? Two hungry friends can't share a meal?" What made her so reluctant to having anything to do with him outside her job?

"Put like that, it does seem silly to say no." She smiled at him.

"Then we have a plan." This type of campaign he could get into.

They were almost back to the starting line when

someone called, "Help! Someone, help!" Rex broke into a run. He came up on a few women on their knees beside another woman, who was lying on the ground.

"I'm a doctor. What's wrong here?" Rex went down on his heels next to the woman.

"She just collapsed," someone said above him.

He checked for a pulse. Finding none, he quickly said, "Someone, call 911 and get the first-aid people." Tilting the woman's head back, Rex checked her airway.

"What can I do?" Tiffani asked from beside him.

"Do you know CPR?"

"Yes," Tiffani said with confidence.

He clasped his hands in the center of the woman's chest. "Then you do the breathing while I do chest compressions. Give her two breaths to start."

Tiffani did as he instructed.

He started chest compressions, Tiffani breathing deeply into the woman's lungs every time he rested, before sitting back as Rex started compressions again.

Tiffani had no idea how long she and Rex worked in unison before the first-aid people arrived. She was in the process of giving the collapsed woman another breath when another woman, carrying an automated external defibrillator bag in hand, knelt beside Rex.

Tiffani, with sweat on her brow, moved out of the way. The tension didn't leave her body as she watched Rex and the woman work.

Rex continued compressions as the first-aid person placed the leads while he talked on the phone. From what she could tell from the conversation, he was talking to the ambulance people.

"Clear!" the woman said, and Rex moved away. Seconds later she pushed a button, sending an electric shock through the patient's body.

Rex leaned his head close to the woman's mouth. "Nothing."

The first-aid woman reset the machine and waited for it to recharge. "Clear!" Once again, she pushed the button. The woman's body jumped.

This time there was a slight coughing sound and the woman's chest started to move.

Tiffani released the breath she hadn't realized she was holding.

The sound of an ambulance's siren filled the air.

The first-aid person slipped an oxygen mask over the patient's nose and mouth.

"Don't move," Rex instructed the patient. To the first-aid person he said, "I'm Dr. Rex Maxwell, by the way. May I use your stethoscope? I'm going to give her a quick check and then I'll get out of the paramedics' way."

The first-aid person handed it over.

Rex efficiently and expertly listened to the patient's heart and lungs. He then checked the pulse in her neck.

Tiffani pulled out her phone and took some pictures. Now that the worst was over, she couldn't miss a chance to capture Rex in action. By the time he was finished the ambulance had arrived. She stood and waited out of the way while Rex spoke to the EMTs.

As the ambulance left, one of the women who had been with the patient said to Rex, "Thank you."

He answered with a warm smile, "Not a problem. I'm just glad I was nearby."

"That's you on the billboard, isn't it?" the woman asked.

"I'm afraid so."

Tiffani smiled at his not-so-gracious admission.

"The hospital picked the right guy. You were a hero today," the woman said.

Looking humbled, Rex nodded and headed toward where Tiffani was standing.

She said as he joined her, "You know, you really are a good guy."

"You doubted it?" He raised an eyebrow.

"Yeah. But it just goes to show you can't believe everything you read." Or believe everything her father had told her about doctors, or what she'd come to believe as true from what had happened with her family. Not all of them were bad. Especially not Rex.

"I could have told you that," he retorted.

Rex had been amazing with the hurt woman. Kind and gentle. He hadn't hesitated to run to help. Giving was part of his nature. All her life, her father had, and still did, demanded her help, always putting his needs first. Rex was just the opposite, thinking of other people before himself. He was so different from what she'd had in her mind he would be.

"Come on," he said. "Let's finish this walk. I'm hungry."

When he took her hand, she let him. The feeling of being wanted, of feeling secure, even if only for five minutes, sped up the healing of her heart.

Half an hour later they were in her car, pulling out into traffic. He gave directions to the restaurant. A short time later they parked in a lot two blocks away and she was shutting her door before Rex could get his legs out.

"I beat you."

"You have me folded up in this clown car and now you're making fun of my manners." He grinned at her.

As they walked to the restaurant Tiffani asked, "Where did those manners come from?"

"My mom said good manners can get you anywhere." He winced as if it had hurt him to confess that but immediately went on, "She reinforced them at home from as far back as I can remember. Cotillions and dance lessons embedded them in me."

"I like them. I'm glad your mother cared enough to teach them to you. Manners make a person think of others before themselves." Something the men in her life had never done as they'd always thought it was about them. She liked having someone think of her first. Even if only to open a door.

As she pondered her new appreciation of simple good manners, he said, "I never thought about it like that." It sounded as if he'd come to an important realization himself. Then he asked, "You ever been to Mac's before?"

"No."

"Best-kept secret in the city." His fondness for the establishment was audible and visible as he stopped in front of a red brick building with a large wooden door. Above it was a sign that read Mac's in bold red letters. Rex held the door open.

She smiled her genuine pleasure as she passed him. "Thank you." Once inside, she turned in time to see his grin and nod of appreciation.

"You're welcome."

They both laughed. She enjoyed laughing with Rex. Hadn't done much of it recently.

They went down a few steps and made a left turn into a dimly lit dining room. Tables were covered in white cloths with small flower vases in the center of each.

"This was a speakeasy during the twenties," Rex informed her on the way to the hostess stand.

"I can imagine." Tiffani loved the place immediately with its warm old-world charm.

A short, heavy-set, balding man came around the stand to greet them, a smile lighting up his face. "Rex. This is a pleasure."

"Hi, Joe," he said, taking the man into a hug and patting him on the back.

They broke apart and Joe said, "Long time no see."

"Too long. I've been busy."

"I saw that. Glad everything worked out," Joe remarked.

Rex stepped back and put his arm around Tiffani's shoulders in a friendly manner, pulling her close. "Joe, I'd like you to meet my friend Tiffani."

Joe's smile deepened. "Hello, Ms. Tiffani."

"Hi." She felt unusually shy all of a sudden.

Rex removed his arm. "Are we too early for the ribs to be ready?"

Joe picked up a couple of menus from the slot on the stand. "Not for you."

"Are they any good?" Rex teased.

"All my ribs are good." Joe grinned as he showed them to a table.

"I'll be the judge of that," Rex declared, pulling a chair out for her.

Tiffani settled into the wooden seat and Rex took the one beside her. Why did he choose to sit so close instead of across from her? Trying to dismiss her uncharacteristic shyness, Tiffani opened her menu. "I'm guessing we don't have to earn his vote of confidence."

"Nope. Joe and I go way back."

"It makes you uncomfortable to talk about the lawsuit, doesn't it?"

A grimace flowed over Rex's face. "I just hate that

people feel they need to tiptoe around what happened. I didn't do anything wrong. I was trying to save the man's life." In the same breath he added, "You're welcome to get anything you want but I recommend the dry-rub rib dinner. You can't go wrong."

Obviously, he was done with that subject. Now that she'd seen him with all sorts of patients she knew there was no way he had ever been guilty of what he'd been accused of. He was passionate about his work, caring. He would have saved that man's life had it been in his power to do so. She shot a covert glance at Rex. Was he the same in other areas of his life?

A young waitress dressed in a white shirt and black skirt came to take their drink orders.

"You eat here often?" Tiffani asked as the waitress walked off.

"No. I wish I did. I stay pretty busy at the hospital."

"I know you're a dedicated doctor and all, but don't you ever do something for fun?"

He shut his menu and put it on top of hers. "Sure I do. Every day."

What was he talking about? "Like what?"

"You won't like my answer. I ride my bike."

Tiffani smirked. "And I'm ruining all your fun."

Rex grinned. "Yeah, you are. I think you should make that up to me."

"And just how should I do that?" She watched as a hint of a wolfish grin curved his lips.

"I have a few ideas." His voice held a provocative note.

Tiffani shifted in her chair. She was grateful when the waitress returned and they ordered the ribs Rex had suggested. When they were alone again she pulled out her phone and announced, "I got some great pictures today. In fact, as soon as we finish here I need to post them."

He ignored the picture on the phone she held out for him to see, keeping his eyes on her face. "You talk about me having fun. What about you? Let's talk about something besides our jobs."

She put her phone away. "Okay, what do you want to talk about?"

"How about what's your favorite movie?"

He kept the easy conversation flowing as the food arrived and they ate. To Tiffani's delight, they had more in common than either of them expected. They even laughed over Rex's story about his first attempt to ride a motorcycle.

"Hey, look this way," Rex said as they finished their meal.

She did as he requested.

He leaned in close and wiped her cheek with a napkin. "You have rub on your face."

Their gazes met, held. Was she imagining the heat swirling around them?

"Well, if it isn't Tiffani Romano," came a sarcastic tone she recognized.

A cold wind blew over her, removing the warmth that had been there only seconds before. The urge to groan grew. *Lou.* What was he doing here? Why was this happening to her? She didn't even want to look. Would it have been so bad for her to have stayed in the heavenly moment Rex had created?

Against her better judgment, she looked up.

"Isn't this a surprise?" Lou said in far too cheerful a voice, his mouth wide with a smile.

"I guess you could call it that." Why couldn't he have just walked on by? More than that, why did she let him get to her? She didn't mean anything to him. All he was trying to do was belittle her to make himself feel more important. He wanted to humiliate her. Again. He made a point of stopping by the office almost daily. She didn't deserve it on her day off as well.

"Funny meeting you here," Lou said.

Tiffani didn't think it was humorous at all. She glanced at the woman with him, who was apparently his newest conquest.

As if she'd given him a reminder to gloat, Lou put his arm around the woman's shoulders and pulled her in so tightly she came off one foot. "This is Monique. She's an up-and-coming model. You may have seen her in a couple of magazines."

Tiffani had. Almost all of her.

She looked at Rex, who must have noticed the anguish in her eyes because he put his arm across the back of her chair and leaned in close. "Honey, aren't you going to introduce me?"

She couldn't deny the pleasure she felt when Lou's smile drooped. "Uh, this is Lou Habersham. A co-worker." She put emphasis on the last word. "Lou, Dr. Rex Maxwell."

"Tiffani, we were more than coworkers," Lou said in a meaningful tone.

"And we aren't anymore." Tiffani felt sorry for Monique, having to listen to this.

Rex smiled and offered his hand. "Your loss is my gain."

Lou looked as if he were taking Rex's hand more out of duty than desire.

"I wish we could ask you to join us but we've just finished our meal and are on our way out. We have something special planned for this afternoon." Rex made the

word *special* sound so suggestive that Tiffani blushed.
That would give Lou his comeuppance. Thanks to Rex,
it now looked like she had a hot doctor and didn't need
him anymore.

Taking her elbow, Rex guided her to her feet. "Enjoy
your meal," he said to Lou, who now looked baffled.

Tiffani gave Monique a reassuring smile. Lou said
nothing. She silently cheered Rex for leaving the pomp-
ous man speechless. As they walked toward the door she
whispered, "Thanks for that."

Rex moved his hand from her elbow to her waist.
"You're welcome."

She appreciated his support. How had he known she'd
needed it?

They paused at the hostess stand, where Rex handed
Joe a few bills. "Ribs were great, Joe. I'll be back soon."

"I'm going to count on that. Bring your lady with
you."

"I'll do that."

She wasn't Rex's lady, but after seeing Lou she
needed to feel like she belonged to him, even if it was
just for a few minutes.

They climbed the stairs and exited. A dark cloud
filled the western sky. There was a roll of thunder before a shower of rain began.

"Do you want to chance it or wait while I go get the
car?" Rex asked.

"I'll walk. I don't want to wait here."

"Okay."

Tiffani headed down the sidewalk. He kept pace with
her but didn't try to take her hand or touch her. As they
went, lightning streaked across the sky and the wind
picked up. The rain grew heavier. He grabbed her hand
and they ran the last of the distance to the car.

Inside it Rex finally asked, "You want to tell me what that was all about back there?"

"It doesn't matter. It was just Lou, being the jerk he is."

"It looked and sounded like more than that." He watched her.

She finally met his gaze. "Rex, I'm sorry. We were having a nice meal. I ruined it and now you're all wet. I'll get you home."

The thunderstorm roared around them.

"I hate wet jeans," Tiffani complained as she started the car. "They stick to you…"

Rex's mouth quirked. "But the view is nice."

Warmth filled her that had nothing to do with the heat coming from the dashboard. Rex had a way of making her feel good about herself, she admitted with reluctance. "I'll have you at your place in a sec. I've already taken up too much of your day."

They rode in silence. They were almost at his apartment when lightning lit the sky just before a heavy roll of thunder followed. The rain made it hard to see in front of them.

"You're not driving home in this. It's too dangerous. Come up to my place until it passes."

"I'll be fine."

"Where do you live?" Rex asked.

"Out toward Germantown."

"That's a good thirty to forty minutes away. More in this weather, and it's headed that direction." He squinted out the windshield.

Fear that if she went into his home she might not want to leave prompted her to protest, "I'm sure you had other plans for your day besides seeing after me."

"Doctor's orders. You're coming in with me."

She couldn't sit around in his house in wet clothes. "I'm a mess. I don't have any spare clothes with me."

"I'll find something you can wear. Stop arguing." When she reached his address he said, "Drive around the block and up the alley. I have a garage there. You can't park on the street in this area."

Tiffani did as he said.

Halfway down the row he instructed, "Let me out here. I'll raise the door."

She watched as he climbed out into the downpour and pulled up the large square metal door. He must feel as miserable as she did in his wet clothes. His back muscles flexed under the soaked, clinging fabric of his T-shirt. He wasn't the only one who could appreciate a view.

Seconds later he was waving her into the garage. His bike was parked there and she pulled in next to it and got out. She stepped into the rain beside him as he pulled the door down in one quick motion. Together they hurried to a single wooden door across the way. Rex pulled keys from his pocket and opened it. Swinging it wide, he let her enter ahead of him.

"Head upstairs. The door at the top is open."

A light came on as she took the first step. The space smelled of oil and lemon, as if the wood had been cared for with polish. She pushed open the door at the top into a spacious kitchen area with brick walls, stainless-steel appliances and an ultra-modern dinning set. The floors were dark hardwood that gleamed even in the dim light. One wall was floor-to-ceiling windows, and beyond that was a roof patio with plants everywhere, even a raised garden. More astonishing was a view of the river.

She turned to Rex. "This is an amazing place."

"I'll let you look around to your heart's desire after you get out of those wet clothes. Come this way and

I'll show you where you can get a shower." He headed down a wide hallway into a huge space that faced the street, visible through four tall windows that lined the front. True to his word, he didn't give her time to explore, leading her to a small hall with two doors leading off it. He went into the one on the right. She followed. He had stopped in the middle of a room that looked as if it doubled as an office and guest room.

He pointed to another door. "There's the bath. Make yourself at home. I'll put some clothes on the doorknob. There's lots of hot water so take your time." He circled her and left, shutting the door behind him.

Rex wondered what possessed him to insist that Tiffani come in. Maybe it was the sad look in her eyes when she'd seen that guy at the restaurant, or the drowned-rat look after they'd jumped into the car, or just that he didn't want her to leave him yet. Whatever it was, he had to live with the decision now.

Tiffani was undressing in his bathroom. He shouldn't have been concerned about having a hot bath because what he really needed was a cold one. Opening a drawer, he selected a T-shirt for her to wear and pulled sweat pants off a hanger in his closet. Going back into his spare room, he hung the clothes on the doorknob of the closed bathroom door.

A sound came from inside. He grinned. Tiffani was singing a pop song. If he didn't get moving, the temptation to ask if he could join her would overcome common sense.

Forcing himself to go to his own bath, he peeled off his wet clothes and stepped under the shower. Minutes later he, dried off and pulled on a fresh T-shirt and a pair of shorts. Gathering his wet clothes, he checked to see if Tiffani was done. Sounds came from the kitchen so he headed that way.

Tiffani stood in her bare feet, looking into a cabinet. She looked so cute, wearing his clothes, even though they were large on her. Her hair was down. The gorgeous tresses fell just below her shoulders.

"I didn't know what I should do with my wet clothes," she said over her shoulder, "so I found the washer and put them in there. Why don't you put yours in with mine and get them going?"

Rex went to the laundry room just off the kitchen to do as she suggested. There was something intimate, almost erotic about the image of their clothes circling and whirling around each other. Rex shook his head. He needed to get control of his thoughts. He returned to the kitchen to find Tiffani looking in a different cabinet.

"Where can I find a glass? I'm thirsty."

"They're over here." He moved beside her and opened a door, reached for a glass and placed it on the counter.

"Thanks."

"It's longer than I thought," he said before he thought.

Tiffani turned. "Uh? What is?"

She pulled self-consciously at the T-shirt he'd given her to wear. "Your shirt?"

Rex stepped closer. "No, your hair." He gave in to his desire to touch it. Though still damp, the smooth strands flowed over his fingers. "Nice."

Tiffani stilled.

He heard her soft intake of breath. His gaze met hers. Her eyes were wide with wonder.

"You've been thinking about my hair?" Her words were almost a whisper.

"Every day since I met you. I've wanted to take it down so many times." He let his palm caress her head.

"Why?"

He shrugged a shoulder. "Because I thought you might let loose some if you let your hair down."

"Why would you want me to do that?"

She really had no idea what he was talking about. As if she couldn't see that she was so wrapped up in her job and her father that she left no room in her life for fun... or a man. He ran his hand beneath her hair at her neck and pulled her toward him. "So you'd be more open to one of these."

His lips found hers. Her arms came around his neck, much to his satisfaction, and she returned his kiss. When she groaned low, he reached around her waist and pulled her against him. It felt right having her there, like he'd been missing her against him since the first day he'd laid eyes on her. His mouth teased hers then traveled over her cheek to nibble behind her ear. Tiffani leaned her head to the side, giving him better access. She purred as he left small kisses along her neck.

"You taste so sweet. Like strawberries and cream," he murmured as his mouth found hers again.

Her fingers traced his nape as she opened her mouth in an invitation that he accepted without hesitation. His tongue entered and greeted hers. She gave him a warm welcome.

She went up on her toes, her body sliding against his. Heat that had been simmering deep inside him boiled over. He hugged her tightly to him. The movements of their meshed mouths turned frantic. He ran his hand over her hip and down to cup one butt cheek. It was every bit as wonderful to touch as it had been to watch in anticipation. He squeezed it, bringing her even closer to his straining manhood. She squirmed with impatience against his length, making him grow harder.

Had he ever been yhis hot for a woman?

He moved his other hand along her side until he brushed her breast beneath the knit material. At her slight press forward of encouragement he cupped her. Tested the weight of the soft mound while running his thumb over her nipple. She wore no bra.

That's right. It was in the washer, mingling with his clothes. She pulled his head closer, her kiss growing more urgent.

He had been right. She was all raw woman beneath the expensive business dress and *appearance was everything* attitude.

Skin. He had to touch hers. His fingers found the hem of the shirt and slipped underneath to touch the warmth and smoothness of her. Had anything ever felt so perfect? Slowly he ran his palms over her back. Tiffani trembled, then deepened her kiss even more than he'd thought possible.

His hands glided up her sides until both hovered near her breasts. Moments later he tenderly followed the curve of a full orb with his fingertips. It was so perfect. Silky. His index finger circled her nipple, found the tip. It stiffened, pushed toward him. He rubbed his palm over it and was rewarded with the feel of it becoming even harder.

Tiffani shuddered.

So responsive. The desire to see her naked, all of her, roared through him. To taste her. To worship her. To have her.

In the back of the burning desire was the knowledge that if he didn't regain control of himself now, he was going to take her on the kitchen floor. But before he could react, Tiffani stepped back, ending their kiss and putting a calming amount of space between them.

CHAPTER SEVEN

WHAT WAS SHE DOING? Tiffani's heart was racing and her hands shaking almost uncontrollably. She'd never acted like a wanton before and here she was in Rex's house, close to begging him to take her. All he'd done was kiss her and she'd lost her mind. "I'm sorry. I really should go."

"Go?" Rex croaked. "What? Why?"

Still unable to meet his look, she stammered, "I... uh... I..."

Rex grabbed her, kissed her again. Hard. Released her. "Please, don't."

She couldn't look at him. What if he ended up treating her the way Lou had? She couldn't survive that kind of devastation again. If she made this step and became too attached and he didn't care for her the same way... But Rex wasn't Lou. He'd proved that over and over. Still...

"You are a client. This is unprofessional."

He lifted her chin with a finger. Her gaze met his. "That has nothing to do with what's going on here. Can't you tell what you do to me? I don't care about anything but that. The rest doesn't matter." Rex studied her for a moment before he adjusted her shirt so it hung around her hips, leaving nothing of her exposed. He tugged on her hand. "Come with me."

"Where are we going?"

"Not where I would like to take you," he said in a droll voice. He led her into the living room to one of the two sofas that faced each other. "Have a seat."

"I really should go. I can get my clothes some other time."

"I can't make you stay, but I wish you would." He stood waiting.

With reluctance, she sat on the edge of the sofa.

Rex came down beside her but not touching her. "I want you to talk to me. I want to understand why you're running from me. The client business is just an excuse."

Tiffani pulled a small sofa pillow into her arms and clutched it to her chest. How could she make him understand how badly she had been hurt? That she was scared to give him the ability to do it too? "Because... I can't—*won't*—let myself be hurt again."

"Where did you get the idea I would hurt you?"

"It's not so much you." How could she explain this to him?

"Does this have something to do with the guy at the restaurant?"

He was always so perceptive. She felt more than saw him watching her intently. "Yeah."

"Will you tell me what happened?" Rex encouraged in a soft tone.

Rex deserved an answer. Yet she hated that Lou was intruding on what had been some of the most wonderful minutes of her life, being in Rex's arms. "I was stupid. I thought I was in love. We'd been dating for six months. I thought we were getting serious. Or at least I was. I'd even taken him to meet my father. Marriage had been mentioned. Then I told him I loved him. That was the end. Turned out he didn't feel the same. What makes it worse is that now he seems to thrive on reminding me. Like today."

"And you think I'd do the same thing?" There was a note of hurt in Rex's voice.

"Yes, no, I don't know. Lou and I work together. You and I basically work together. This campaign is important. Even now our relationship has become more personal than it should."

"Do you trust me?" Rex asked, taking one of her hands.

She nodded.

"Do you think I'd ever do anything to intentionally hurt you?"

"No." And she was confident he wouldn't.

"Good. I can't guarantee what will happen in the future but I can tell you about the here and now. There is something special between us, something I haven't shared with another woman. I can't put a name to it because I'm not sure what it is, but I know it's strong. Worth exploring. I want to know you in all the ways I can. Enjoy you. I'm willing to see what happens, if you are."

Tiffani hesitated, so Rex carried on.

"I understand the campaign and the chance for the promotion is important to you. I respect that." He continued to play with her fingers as he leaned back on the sofa and twisted sideways to face her, bending his knee to bring his leg up on the cushions.

He was saying all the right things. "I promised myself I wouldn't have another office romance or let myself get carried away again…"

"It doesn't take much for us to get carried away," Rex said with a grin.

"No, it doesn't." She looked at him from beneath her lashes.

Rex gave her a sly grin. "I like it when you get carried away. Those sweet moans, your touches and kisses. Look at me, Tiffani."

She did, against her better judgment.

"If we'd kept going the way we were in the kitchen, I would've had you on the floor in two more seconds. You deserve better than that. I want to make sure we're on the same page. I never want you to regret being with me, or being honest about your feelings."

Despite what she had said about being careful, her half-healed heart opened and took him in. He was thinking about her. Not what he needed or what she could do for him, but what was best for her. She'd had that so rarely in her life. Since she'd been young it had always been about helping her mother, her father, her family. With Lou it had been all about him. "Thank you for that."

"I'm going to make you a promise right now. I'll always be honest with you and will never hide who I am from you. What you see is what you get. Okay?"

She nodded.

"Now, with your permission, I'm going to show you just how amazing I think you are."

If she took this chance, she was opening the door to pain—but if she didn't, what would she miss out on? The possibility of something wonderful with Rex. She was going to take the chance. "Okay."

He pulled her onto his lap, his mouth taking hers. Their tongues danced as his hand made a path through her hair.

Tiffani met him kiss for kiss. She wanted this. If there was fallout with her job she would deal with it.

Her heart would be hard to handle but she would face that when and if it happened. Rex had made her promises and she trusted him.

He released her mouth and sat back. "This has to go," he said, tugging at her T-shirt.

"The windows. Daylight," she muttered through her stupor. The rain was still pounding against them, but they were exposed nevertheless.

"No one is going to see us. And I can't imagine anything more beautiful than you naked in the light. Your body should never be hidden."

A shot of delight went through her to know Rex desired her so much.

He raised her hands, skimming the shirt off. Tiffani cupped his face, brushed his hair away and with a gentle tug brought his lips to hers. Into her kiss she put all her passion. He pulled back and gave her a wicked look that started a pulsating need deep in her center. "You keep that up and I might not be accountable for what I do next."

"I might like that."

With all the confidence she'd heard more than once when he talked to his patients, he said, "I can guarantee it. But right now I want to admire you."

He dropped his gaze to her breasts. His hands tenderly caressed them, making them tingle. She hissed in pleasure when the pads of his thumbs massaged her nipples. They rose hard and erect as if straining for more of his caresses. The pulsating in her center began to grow. She held her breath as his head moved lower.

His warm, wet mouth covered a nipple. Letting her head fall back, she closed her eyes and relished the wave of hot desire rolling through her. As Rex's tongue circled then softly tugged, her center contracted. She squirmed, needing more. So much more. And soon.

He lingered, her tip remaining in his mouth. The pressure between her legs intensified. Rex took the other breast and gave it equal loving attention. How he pulled such feeling from her was a mystery she didn't care to solve. The cool air on her wet breast sent a shiver through her that quickly became a quiver of increasing need.

She feared she was going to spiral off into space too soon. His arousal pressed hard against her hip. She shifted, rubbing against it, eliciting an animal sound from him. As Rex suckled, he nudged her back on the sofa. His hand returned to fondle her other breast as his mouth continued working its magic.

Tiffani opened her eyes and pushed his hair away so she could watch. A sense of wonder filled her. This gorgeous, intelligent and uncommon man was loving her. She'd never been this hot for a man's touch.

His hand slipped from her breast and caressed the outside of her thigh then up and over it. He shifted her so he could touch where she was hot and wanting. He rubbed the fabric covering the juncture of her thighs back and forth. She closed her eyes and savored the erotic sensation, heat bubbling within.

Rex raised his eyes. Their gazes met and held as he shifted on top of her, the ridge of his desire barred from her center by clothing. She writhed.

"Tiff, you are so amazing. Do you feel what you do to me?" He flexed against her.

She ran her hands over his chest and down to the hem of his shirt. Slipping her hands beneath it, she caressed his heated skin. Wanting more, she pushed his shirt up until he sat on his knees and yanked it over his head.

Tiffani reveled in the sight of so much of masculine flesh on view just for her. He lowered himself once more and she traced a fingertip over one of his ribs.

He hissed as she continued to explore the line of hair disappearing under the waistband of his shorts. His mouth claimed hers as their skin met.

No man before Rex had ever set her nerve endings on overload like this.

His kiss was gentle, almost reverent. Giving. Reassuring.

While he began dropping small kisses along her cheek, he pushed at the sweat pants he'd loaned her. She shifted, helping him to shove them from her hips and tug them to her knees. He rolled to his side and his palm found the plane of her belly. Leisurely, he moved his fingers over her skin, studying and surveying, slowly moving downward to brush the curls.

Tiffani watched as Rex explored her body. His eyes abruptly rose to meet hers. "So beautiful."

Everything he'd said and done in these last almost eternal moments were like a balm to her wounded soul. He made her believe she was significant to his world.

She guided his lips to hers. Kissed him with gentle appreciation.

His finger found her bare center and teased her entrance. She moaned. Every fiber of her being was focused on his next action.

With one smooth move he slipped his finger inside her. She involuntarily flexed toward him. He exited and entered, repeating it with increasing speed until Tiffani thought she wasn't going to survive the excruciating bliss. Heat built, flamed, until it roared in her ears.

Without warning, it back-flashed, spiraling into a tower that bore her high. Gently she floated in a cloud of ecstasy that brought her softly back to reality.

Blinking, she registered she was naked in the daylight on Rex's sofa while he smiled down at her.

He whispered, "That was the most stunning sight I've ever seen. Thank you for letting me be a part of it."

How could she not love a man like him? But she would never say that aloud.

The moment Tiffani had found her pleasure by his hand, something changed in Rex. No one had ever let go so totally or readily for him. She still had him tied up in knots of need for his own release but he'd found joy in just watching her. Something beyond his understanding was happening between them.

He didn't have women to his place. Didn't have sex in his living room in the daylight. Didn't bring people involved in his work life into his personal world. He was at a loss for what to think.

What had made him scrap all his standards and beliefs?

Tiffani.

He looked down at her, lying half beneath him. She was watching him with a shy expression. "Thank you, Rex. For that wonderful…" She waved her hand. Her fingertips brushed his chest and his manhood jumped. Her eyes widened for a fraction of a second. "And for making me feel special."

He shifted, letting her know he still desired her. "You are special."

Seconds later she pulled her legs from beneath him. Kicking off her pants, she stood before him. There was nothing unsure about her direct look. She reached out her hand. He took it. Tiffani led him toward the bedrooms. When she started into the one she knew he pulled her hand. "Mine."

She took the lead again, taking him to the edge of his bed and stopping. Looking him straight in the eyes, she pushed at the waistband of his shorts until they dropped to the floor. She stepped back and studied his manhood straining stone hard toward her. Her gaze wandered over his chest before her look met his again. The tip of her fingers caressed the top of one shoulder.

When was the last time he'd quivered with need like this? Had he ever?

"You're too much. Too male. Too gorgeous. Too sexy. Too caring," she whispered, as she took hold of his waist then came up on her toes to kiss him. The second he tried to take her in his arms she stilled him but continued to build the heat in him by nibbling kisses along his mouth. She took his bottom lip between her teeth, giving it a gentle squeeze.

Releasing his mouth and hands, she grasped his forearms and turned him so his back was to the bed. He started to wrap his arms around her but she pushed them away. "Not yet. It's still my turn."

That was the Tiffani he recognized. The one in control, who knew what she wanted and would get it. The strong, self-assured person, not the sad, beaten one he'd seen earlier. He liked her vulnerable side that needed him but this bold one was hot, set his blood on fire.

"Lie back on the bed." She gave his chest a gentle shove with the palm of her hand. He fell back onto the mattress. Seconds later she was beside him. Her hand roamed his chest as she planted kisses along the crest of his shoulder. Again he attempted to touch her but she wouldn't allow it. "No, this is my turn."

Frustration built in him like pressure in a volcano.

Her fingers found his hair and brushed it out around his head. "I love your hair. All wild and wonderful."

"I thought you wanted it cut short," he said with a grin.

Tiffani leaned back so that he could see her face clearly. "No. I think you're like Samson, you get your strength from it. It's a statement of who you are." She threaded her fingers through his and stretched her arms out. Letting her breasts sweep his chest, she gave him a wet, hot kiss.

Rex's restraint was close to his limit. She straddled him and every muscle in his body constricted. His manhood rested in the crease of her behind. Just one small movement...

She rose up on her knees. "Protection?"

"Drawer," he croaked, and pointed to his bedside table.

Tiffani leaned over him. After pulling the drawer open, she rummaged around until she came out with a square package. He took it from her, opened it and quickly covered himself. He fisted a handful of her hair and brought her mouth back to his.

As they kissed Tiffani positioned her moist, hot center over him. Slowly, agonizingly slowly, she slid down his shaft. Rex clenched his teeth at the exquisite pleasure. He couldn't have stopped the lift of his hips if he'd wanted to. With one swift surge she took his entire length. Her eyes closed as an enraptured look covered her face. She pulled upward and pushed down again. When she started to repeat it, he met her action with an instinctive reaction.

She pulled her mouth from his and straightened,

throwing back her head, hands braced on his chest as their pace became more frantic. He watched her breasts bobbing, keeping time with their joined rhythm. He would remember this view forever.

Tiffani's mouth formed a small O, as if this second orgasm had taken her by surprise. She shuddered over him.

Male satisfaction filled him. He felt like he should be standing at the top of a mountain, thumping his chest, letting all the world know how great a lover he was.

She eased down over his chest like melting ice cream in the sunshine and sighed.

He rolled her over and reentered her. Gathering his hair in her hands and wrapping her legs around his waist, she joined him in his frantic ride to the finish. With a low grunt of release, he was transported to paradise.

Rex didn't know what time it was when he woke but there was still daylight and he was sprawled out on the top of his bed with the most amazing woman he'd ever met curled into his side, sleeping.

It had been a surreal day. Nothing had been as he'd expected. Tiffani had made it different. There was movement beside him. He looked at her. Her eyelids rose slowly. She blinked and her eyes went round.

"Hey," she said shyly, and looked away.

"Hey, yourself."

She shifted away from him and climbed off the bed.

He reached for her and just missed her hand. "Where're you going?"

"I should find my clothes."

Rex watched her bare butt as she exited his room. This unsure Tiffani was a new side of her he found intriguing.

A few seconds later, as he was pulling on his shorts

he saw her dashing into the other bedroom with clothes in her arms. So much for the soft afterglow moments. Did she regret what had happened between them? He wasn't going to let the situation become awkward. What they had shared had been amazing, nothing to be was ashamed of.

He was in the kitchen when Tiffani showed up again, wearing the clothes he'd let her borrow. He informed her, "I put our clothes in the dryer. They should be done in a little while. I thought you might like a glass of tea while you wait." He sat the two cups on the table.

"I don't think I'll wait for my clothes. I'll get them later." She moved toward the door.

"Whoa." He grabbed her forearm. "Where're you headed?"

She looked at his hand and he let it fall away. "I just think it's time for me to go."

Rex stepped close to her. "Take a breath. Slow down. Why don't you have a seat and we can talk about any arguments you might have to me kissing you again." He grinned at her and pulled out a chair. "Because I'm certainly going to kiss you again."

She gave him an odd but endearing smile before she dropped into the chair. A few seconds later she took a sip of tea.

Rex sat at the end of the table to give her some space. She appeared to relax. The silence, to his surprise, wasn't tense but more like that of two friends sharing a few quiet moments.

"This sure is a nice kitchen," she said, looking around. "It looks like it's used regularly. Some woman isn't going to come home and find me here, is she?"

Her sense of humor was starting to return. "You're asking me *now* if I have a wife or girlfriend?"

"I know you don't. Remember I read your bio." She played with the condensation on the glass.

He nodded. "That's right, the big folder of doom."

She cracked a smile.

Progress. He wanted the fun and open Tiffani back. "For your information, I do the cooking here. I consider myself a gourmet chef when I have time to prepare a meal."

"Really?"

He smiled. "That wasn't in the folder of doom either."

Her eyes lit up. "No, but that's great information. I could really use it."

"Tiff, I didn't tell you that so you can use it for the campaign. Can't you be off work for a little while?"

"I'm sorry. It's really all I have and I sometimes get carried away." She looked both sincere and sad.

Rex turned serious. "If I tell you something few others know, are you going to tell the world?"

She wrinkled her nose. "I might want to but I'll keep it to myself. So what is it?"

Satisfaction ran through him. He'd captured her attention. "I grow most of my food."

"I noticed your garden outside. That's really wonderful." She walked to the glass door and looked out onto his rainy patio. "Did you learn to cook from your mom?"

"Hardly. We had a housekeeper. My mother was too busy spending her time at the country club and planning bridge parties to cook."

Tiffani's attention came back to him. Had she heard the bitterness in his voice? "My daddy wouldn't have a garden. He could have. People offered to build boxes high enough for him but he didn't want anyone's help."

"You would've liked to have had a garden, wouldn't you? I learned to cook by watching late-night cooking shows to wind down after a long day. The cooks talked about using fresh vegetables and herbs and I thought I'd give it a try. Turns out I'm good at it."

"You're good at a lot of things."

He gave her a lopsided grin and a pointed look. "I like to think so."

Tiffani blushed a lovely shade of pink. "I'm just going to get my clothes. If they're a little damp it won't matter. I'm sure the good-looking bachelor must have a date on a Saturday night."

She didn't wait for him to respond before she headed for the laundry room.

That was it! Rex followed her. "Let me get this right. You actually think that I'd have sex with you in the afternoon and go out on a date this evening? You think that little of me?"

Tiffani straightened from where she had been looking into the dryer. She clutched a couple of articles of clothing in her hands. "I don't know what I think. I hadn't planned on this afternoon happening."

Rex stepped closer. "I didn't either." His hands came to rest on her waist. "But I thought it was amazing. More than amazing." He placed kisses along her neck.

"I need—"

He brought her against his growing manhood, letting her know what he was thinking. He murmured, "What do you need?"

Her mouth found his. The clothes she held fell to the floor as her arms circled his neck. Rex lifted her and she wrapped her legs around his hips. Taking a step back, he set her on the top of the dryer. She let him go and shimmied out of her pants while he pushed his shorts down and kicked them away. His lips found hers again.

He could learn to love this Tiffani.

* * *

The next morning the sun streamed through Tiffani's bedroom window. The storm had passed. She moved and a sweet soreness reminded her she had used muscles for activities she hadn't enjoyed for far too long. Sex on a dryer. That was a new one for her. One she'd like to repeat.

Her lack of control yesterday still shocked her. But she'd loved every second of touching and being touched by Rex. Her body heated at just the thought of him. She didn't know how she would concentrate on the campaign now. Whenever she was around him all she'd be thinking about was finding a place where they could be alone.

He'd not asked her to stay the night. She was glad because she wasn't sure she could have said no. And the way she'd acted like a loved-starved ninny who had never had a man look at her was still horribly embarrassing. But she hadn't ever had a man look at her the way Rex had. He was the first *real* man she'd ever been with.

Intelligent, caring, attentive, as interested in her pleasure as his own, giving and fun. How had she been so wrong about him? Worse, how could she have let things between them become personal? A real relationship between them would never work. There were too many variables working against them. His job, hers. Him in Memphis and her wanting to move away. Her betraying her father. Rex had said nothing about ever wanting to settle down. He was, she assured herself, the love-them-and-leave-them type. All they'd done yesterday had been to create a big tangle.

From now on any interaction between them would be strictly business. Tiffani groaned in despair, but his kiss goodbye last night had been perfect. For a second, she would have sworn she had floated.

But no more thinking like that.

She climbed out of bed. Enough of the daydreaming. Her father was expecting her to visit. She wouldn't disappoint him. He had called, asking her to do some shopping for him.

If she didn't discipline herself, she'd stay in bed and relive every second of those moments with Rex.

The last few days were ones to remember, but not in a good way. They didn't improve when Rex's cellphone rang around seven that evening as he pushed open the hospital door leading to the parking lot with thoughts of calling Tiffani.

"Rex Maxwell," he answered, trying not to snap but just missing it.

"Dr. Maxwell, you're needed in the OR. Auto accident."

He sighed. "I'm on my way."

Despite his regular surgery schedule, he'd done his share of emergency surgery in the last few days. He hadn't even had time to call or see Tiffani. He only hoped she didn't think he had used her and forgotten about her. He didn't believe in being intimate with a woman and then ignoring her. The least he would do was explain how he felt if he didn't plan to see her again. In Tiffani's case, he had every intention of seeing more of her, as well as experiencing her.

The problem was he couldn't get away from the hospital. He didn't remember another time he'd resented his job but he did tonight. Tiffani pulled at him. Like a need he didn't think would ever be fulfilled. But right now he had a job to do.

He hurried up the stairs to the second floor. Pushing

through the surgery suite doors, he asked the unit secretary which OR.

She called as he continued down the hall toward the locker room, "Six."

Minutes later he was changed, back in scrubs and washing his hands.

His scrub nurse came up beside him with a hat and mask. He leaned down and she helped him finish dressing. "So, what do we have?"

In a solemn voice she said, "Teen. One-car accident. Rollover. Thrown out. Internal injuries."

Rex let out a string of expletives beneath his mask.

"I know what you mean," his nurse replied. "It seems like it happens every full moon." She looked closely at Rex. "When was the last time you slept in your own bed and not in an on-call room?"

"Three or four nights ago," he said, remembering how Tiffani had left and he'd wished he'd insisted she stay. But he hadn't wanted to push. She was skittish enough about them being together. He'd missed her all night long. "Anesthesia ready?"

"Will be by the time we get in there." His nurse finished tying his mask.

"Then let's go."

They headed into the OR.

"History?" he said to his physician's assistant, who was already standing beside the patient on the table.

"Sixteen-year-old male, good heath, no allergies. Only issue is that his car didn't win the war with the tree."

"Let's get him patched up. What're we going after first?" Rex glanced at the X-rays on the wall screen.

"Spleen," the PA said.

"Turn on the rock 'n' roll and let's get started." Rex

stepped to the table. The music filled the room as he removed the organ, stitched up two perforations to the boy's kidney, one to the stomach. He had hopes of closing when the monitors started beeping.

"BP's going down," the anesthesiologist said urgently from by the patient's head.

"There has to be a bleeder somewhere. Suction." Tension started to well in him. He needed to find it, and fast.

Over the next few minutes he searched frantically with no success. Rex was still looking when the anesthesiologist said, "That's it."

"Continue CPR while I look," Rex demanded.

"It's over, Rex." The anesthesiologist met his look over his mask and shook his head. "He was already too far gone when he came in."

That wasn't what the family was going to want to hear. Rex left the OR. In the locker room, he jerked off his cap and slung it to the floor. Sitting on the bench, he put his forearms on his knees and hung his head. Now he had to go tell the boy's parents he'd been unable to save his life. These cases took a bite out of his heart every time.

Had he done all he could do? What had he missed? Should he have made the repairs in a different order? For all his bravado about it, before the lawsuit he'd never questioned himself like he did now. It was hard to admit, but it was true.

Picking up his cap, he stood and headed for the waiting room. Talking to the parents couldn't be put off any longer.

CHAPTER EIGHT

IT HAD BEEN easier to avoid crossing paths with Rex than Tiffani had anticipated. Sunday she had spent with her father. It hadn't been pleasant. He'd harped on about her job being a betrayal of her loyalty to him. She knew she mustn't ever let escape the least hint of how she'd spent her afternoon the day before. Even so, her father noticed her mind wandered more often than usual.

The next three long days at the office she spent managing social media, a magazine interview and other details of the campaign. Rex must have decided, as she had, that what they had done couldn't continue, because he hadn't tried to contact her. She didn't have a good reason to call him so she left things well enough alone. Yet he was constantly in her thoughts. When she wasn't dreaming of being kissed by him, she was forced to speak his name in the course of her job.

Her doorbell ringing just before midnight woke her. Someone needing something this late couldn't be good. Her phone buzzed, indicating a text message. What was going on?

She looked at her phone.

The doorbell rang again.

The number was Rex's.

Let me in.

Her heart hummed. Her common sense balked. Why was he here? It didn't matter. He just was.

She didn't bother with a robe and hurried downstairs in her nightshirt. Flipping on the porch light, she checked through the peephole. He was leaning against the doorjamb. The doorbell rang again. She unlocked the door. "What's wrong? Are you hurt?"

There was a weariness that hung heavily around him. His shoulders slumped. Concern pushed away any excitement she felt over seeing him. "Tell me what's wrong. What happened?"

He wrapped her in his arms and buried his face in her neck. "I don't want to think about it. Talk about it. I just want us. To know again how good you make me feel." His mouth found hers. There was hunger, desperation and need in his movements. His tongue mated with hers, becoming more desperate with every thrust.

All her vows fled. The glow only he could ignite with his touch grew. Sheer joy filled her. Her nerves tingled and her heart hammered against her ribs. This was what being alive felt like! She had no fear other than that Rex might pull away. He was hurting and she was here for him.

He lifted her and carried her inside far enough to kick the door closed, holding her so tight her breath was erratic. His mouth found her earlobe and his teeth bit down until she winced. With a brush of the tip of his tongue, he eased the pain. He cupped her butt and jerked her against him. His manhood was thick, long and solid beneath the fabric of his scrubs.

"I need you," he growled, then kissed her neck. "Now."

She sensed his desperate fight for control more than

felt it. To know she'd driven him so close to his breaking point empowered her femininity, set her own desire to boil deep inside her. Blood rushed to her center, to where she urgently craved Rex.

He needed *her*. Had come to find her.

Happiness gushed within her. She brought her legs up around his hips. "My bedroom is upstairs."

His hands tightened on her hips before he walked toward the stairs.

"Too far." Those two words were a snarl of feral need.

He set her on a step and came over her, kissing her again while delving under her sleepshirt and giving her panties an urgent tug. Seconds later they were wrapped around her ankles. Rex let go long enough to pull a package from his pocket and pull his pants down. He rolled on his protection, braced his hands on the step her shoulders lay against. He looked at her, studied her a second as if asking permission. She nodded, and without hesitation he pushed into her.

She accepted all of him. Something horrible must have happened, because the caring man who had been so tender a few days earlier was gone. In his place was this frantic, wild man who had come to her for solace. The wonder of his transformation amazed and gratified her with a profoundness that made her steady herself against his forearms and accept his strong thrusts readily. She would be sore in the morning but that didn't matter. Rex needed her, and she wanted him.

With one final plunge, he shook and grunted his release. He came down on top of her, his head resting on her breast and sighed. "Tiff."

She wrapped her arms around him and held him tight. "I'm right here. It'll be all right."

Tiffani was slowly rubbing circles on his back when

he shifted off her. Rex now seemed embarrassed or
ashamed, or perhaps both. She felt honored he'd chosen
her to smooth away his pain. The self-assured surgeon
had been vulnerable, and had come to her for accep-
tance.

He searched her face. She let her concern for him,
for his wellbeing, shine through her eyes as she met
his. Standing, he pulled up his pants. She wanted to say
something but nothing appropriate came to mind. Rex
offered her his hand and she took it. He helped her to
her feet. Tiffani wobbled for a second and he put a hand
on her elbow. Her panties remained hooked on one foot.

He went down on his knees and stretched the tiny
piece of hot pink material. "Step in." She did as he asked.
With careful, gentle movements, he pulled them up and
into place. That was almost as erotic as what had just
happened.

"Please, forgive me. There is no excuse for that kind
of behavior." He put his back to her as he stood. "I…I
should go. I was wrong to come here. To take my bad
day out on you."

"Don't."

He looked at her. "I'm surprised you're not screaming
at me. I barge in here, wouldn't tell you why, and took
you on the stairs? A few minutes ago I was only thinking of myself. That's not how it should be between us."

"I could tell you were hurting. You would never hurt
me, remember? I believe that. I was glad I was here
for you. I understand." She paused and smiled. "And I
liked it too."

Her words were like a balm to Rex's wounded heart.

This time she was the one who reached out a hand.
He took it and she led him up the stairs.

He hadn't planned to come to Tiffani's. Somehow,

he'd found himself speeding through the streets and had ended up here. If he hadn't remembered the detail about the flower pot she kept beside her front door he might still be wandering the city. No, he would have called her. He'd needed Tiffani. She had made the devastated faces of the family of the boy he'd lost go away for a few minutes.

"The bathroom is in there." She pointed to a door off her room. "Go have a hot shower. Have you eaten anything?"

"Not since noon." He sounded tired even to himself.

"Then while you're getting a shower, I'll fix you something to eat." She headed for the door.

Some of the shame Rex felt eased. She should have put him out on his tail for the way he had behaved, but instead she had shown him concern.

Half an hour later, Rex went down her stairs wearing only his scrub pants. A soft humming told him in what direction to go to find Tiffani. She had her back to him as he stood in the doorway of the kitchen, watching the gentle movements of her hips as she worked at the counter.

This was a sight he could get used to. A sight he could look forward to coming home to.

"Hey."

She smiled over her shoulder.

"Thanks for the shower. I didn't leave any hot water."

"You weren't supposed to." She picked up a plate and put it on the table in front of the chair closest to him. On it was a ham sandwich, some apple slices and chips.

"Not a gourmet meal like you can fix but the best I can do this late at night. Tea will be ready in a minute." She stepped to the stove. "Have a seat. Don't wait for me."

Rex pulled the chair out from the small white table and sat. "This looks good."

The teapot whistled and Tiffani picked it up and poured water into the two mugs waiting on the counter. Each had a tea bag string hanging over the side. "My mother always said hot tea makes everything feel a little bit better."

She sat a mug in front of him then gingerly took a chair at the end of the table. Placing her mug on the table as well, she sat and cradled it with both hands, as if warming them.

Guilt swamped him. He picked up half of the sandwich. Tiffani had actually cut it in half. He'd not had that done for him since he was a child. She had a way of making him feel cared for. She'd demonstrated that more than once while working at the clinic and had certainly shown him in the aftermath of his self-induced shame a short while ago. It had been a long time since he'd felt special to anyone. Her generosity tonight was more than he deserved. He took a bite of the sandwich. "This is good. Thank you."

"Despite your gourmet cook status, I don't think you take good enough care of yourself. You miss too many meals."

"Now you sound like a doctor or a nagging wife."

She sat straighter, looking indignant. "I'm neither, thank you."

He liked the fire in her eyes. Finishing his sandwich and chips, Rex started on his apple slices, pausing for a sip of tea. The warmth did calm him somewhat.

Tiffani twisted the handle of her mug one way then

the other before she said, "Will you tell me what happened to upset you?"

Rex stopped crunching his apple. After the way he had acted he owed her some explanation. His gaze met hers. Everything about hers said she wouldn't accept silence. "I'm sorry about tonight. I shouldn't have done that."

"I'm glad I was here for you," she answered in a soft voice. "Please, tell me why I needed to be."

It took all that was in him to show his weakness but she deserved to know what had driven him to come to her. "I lost a teenager tonight. I hate telling parents their child is gone. There was nothing I could do."

She didn't touch him, just said softly, "You and I know better than most that not everyone can be fixed. You even said that during the interview the other day."

She was right.

"Yeah, but that doesn't make it better, or any easier."

"No, it doesn't." Reaching across the table, she gave his hand a squeeze. "Knowing how you feel, the malpractice case must have been especially tough on you."

It had been. More than he'd let on to himself, and nothing he would show the world. It had caused doubt to creep in. Made him second-guess, analyze every decision he made in a case. He went over and over them in his head, looking for something he could have done differently.

Tiffani continued, "I didn't read much about the case on purpose. I didn't want to judge you any more than I already had. You were the center point of the campaign and I wanted to think forward, but I did hear some of the media reports."

"They were neither flattering or accurate. Especially

with the Royster family doing all the talking." He pulled his hand from hers.

It might kill him to tell the story but he was going to anyway. After how he'd acted with Tiffani she deserved to know the monsters that chased him. "I don't know if it was the fates, the universe getting back at me or just the luck of the draw that my patient turned out to be Mr. Royster."

Without saying anything, Tiffani's look asked him to explain. He had her complete attention. She even stopped fiddling with her mug.

"Vic Royster used to be my father's best friend when I was growing up. He was also the father of my girlfriend in high school."

Tiffani pursed her lips and nodded. "I thought doctors avoided doing surgery on people they were friends with?"

"I had no idea it was him. I was called in. An emergency. I didn't know the patient's name until after I was out of surgery. He was already too far gone by the time I got to him. I couldn't have done anything more than I did. But I did try." Talking about that night started the sick feeling he remembered so well churning his guts once again. Would it ever go away?

"So why the lawsuit?"

He looked at her. "The problem was, my past came back to haunt me."

Tiffani regarded him with expectation.

He was going to have to tell her about his dirty laundry as well. She shouldn't have to hear it but it was part of his story. "When I was a kid I lived in a world of affluence. My family lived in the nicest neighborhood, had the best cars. Even traded each year for the newest model. I wore the best brands from the best stores in town. We were members of the most renowned country club. I attended the most prestigious private school. We were in the 'in crowd.'"

"So that's where the great manners came from," Tiffani commented.

"That had a lot to do with it. I attend cotillion classes and there were dances all the time. At home, the social graces were required. It was important to always look and act correctly. My mother was very particular. To her, manners were a reflection of breeding. Appearance was everything."

He took a sip of his now-cold tea. "I was a senior in high school when I found out that all my family lived on was nothing but a house of cards. I discovered that only when it collapsed. Big time. My father and mother had had us living a lie. They were living far beyond their means. We had been part of a lifestyle they couldn't afford and it finally caught up with them. My dad had to file for bankruptcy. Gone were the house, the cars, the clothes and the friends. Do you have any idea how fast so-called friends can disappear when you embarrass them?"

Tiffani didn't answer. Just looked at him with steady, almost unreadable eyes. Thankfully her gaze didn't hold pity. If it had, he might have left.

Shaking his head and focusing on his tea mug, he forced himself to continue. "The country-club life was over. We moved across town to a three-bedroom apartment in an area our old friends wouldn't even drive through. Mr. Royster wouldn't take my father's calls. My girlfriend, the one I foolishly hoped to marry, told me she couldn't associate with a penniless person. She had to think about the repercussions of even being seen with me."

Tiffani hissed in a manner that reminded him of the sound a mother might make when her child was in danger. Her knuckles were white from where she now gripped her mug.

"What we didn't do was change schools. The year was already paid for. It would have been better if we had. Those last few months for me and my brother were horrible.

"I came out of the experience promising myself that I'd never put on the pretense of being more important than anyone else. I swore to myself I'd never use my job, my house, clothes or what I drive to create a façade of self-importance. I was going to be me and no one else."

"So the long hair, jeans and calling you by your first name comes from that." Tiffani was speaking more to herself as if she at last had found answers to her questions.

"Yep, what you see is what you get. Like it or not."

"So how did you afford to go to medical school?"

He shrugged. "I had good grades. I was always good at math and got great experience working in the nursing home. I received some scholarships, took out some loans and worked like hell. I was determined not to give up my dreams because my parents had selfishly pretended to be different people without considering the consequences if the truth came out. I like knowing I earned what I had." He sighed. "Anyway, Mr. Royster just showed up in my OR. When I had to go out and tell Mrs. Royster and her daughter, my old girlfriend, that he had passed away, I hadn't seen them in over fifteen years. Unsurprisingly, it wasn't a happy reunion."

"I can only imagine."

"They couldn't accept his death was natural. Couldn't accept he'd not been taking good care of himself or that he should have seen a doctor sooner. They blamed me for his death. They had the money and status to bring the lawsuit. At one point, they even accused me of letting Mr. Royster die on purpose because I wanted revenge for how he'd turned his back on my family when I was a kid. I think that will hurt more than anything for a very long time. These were people who had known me for a significant portion of my life and yet they actually thought I was low enough to let him die out of *revenge*."

Rex shook his head. He was almost done. "With the lawsuit involving both me and the hospital, I wasn't able to say anything. I was told to keep my mouth shut. But the Roysters could say anything they wanted, and took every opportunity to do so. Even airing my own mother and father's bankruptcy and fall from high social grace all those years ago."

"Oh, no," Tiffani said.

"I didn't agree with what my parents did but I certainly didn't want to see them dragged through the mud because of me."

"I'm sorry all of that happened to you." He hated the sad look that now filled her eyes.

"Yeah, but it's over and done now. I've moved on."

She gave him a dubious look but didn't question him further, for which he was grateful.

Tiffani's heart hurt for him. He'd suffered. In her opinion, he still was, but he couldn't see that about himself. She stood and went behind him. Putting her arm around his neck, she put her hands over his heart. It beat strong and hard, just like he was. He was a survivor who could still give to others. She pushed back his hair and kissed his temple. "You know, you're the biggest-hearted person I know. I love you because you care." She realized what she'd said too late. "Uh, you know what I mean."

Rex clasped her hands just as she started to withdraw. "I know what you mean," he said, sounding profoundly grateful. "Thank you for being here for me. Listening." He turned in his chair and pulled her down to sit in his lap.

Her arm went around his shoulders and she kissed him.

Sometime later he whispered against her ear, "I know I probably don't deserve it, but I'd like to stay tonight if you'll let me."

Tiffani stood. Taking his hand, she led him toward the stairs. "Come on. You need your rest."

The sun was high in the sky when she awoke. Rex's head rested on her shoulder. When they had come to bed he'd just held her. It had been as if he'd needed to feel someone was there for him. She was glad he had picked her.

Although she needed to call work, she wasn't willing to take the chance she might wake Rex to do so. Running her hand over his hair, she marveled that he lay in her arms. Rex was fast becoming important to her. Too much so. Forever with him was easy to imagine. If it was only that simple. Their lives were here and now, only for the moment. They had no real tomorrows, were on two different paths.

She'd had such a negative view of doctors all her life. Rex had learned to mistrust people. Her job was to make people look better. He despised any pretense. She was buttoned up and he was let your hair down. She was leaving and he was staying. It was impossible. All she could do was enjoy this all-too-brief interlude.

The fingertips of his hand skimmed across the skin of

her waist. Her pulse quickened. Rex was waking up. He rolled over and kissed the top of one breast before looking up at her to murmur, "Softest pillow I've ever had."

"I need to call work. I'm late." Tiffani moved to untangle herself from him.

"Don't go in today. Let's do something fun. Laugh." He gave her an imploring look as his fingers brushed over her skin.

"I can't, I have to work." Tiffani hated telling him no.

"You can call it a day of work. I'll let you take pictures. I'll even help an old lady across the street so you'll have something for social media." He grinned, the one that could get her to do almost anything.

She returned it. "You're a funny man so early in the morning."

"Come on, Tiff, live on the wild side a little bit." He was serious.

This was another area where they were so different. He didn't take his life too seriously. Knew how to laugh at himself. Enjoy living. "Okay, funny man. What do you think we ought to do?"

He sat up and looked at her with a twinkle in his eye. "How about a visit to Elvis's house? Ever been there?"

"Yes, but it's been a long time." This was the last suggestion she would have expected from him.

"Then Graceland here we come." He popped out of bed. "Shower, my place for a change of clothes and breakfast, then we're on our way."

Tiffani couldn't help but laugh. He was a completely different person from the one who had shown up on her doorstep the night before. She liked both sides of Rex. The tough, hardened one and the one who reminded her of a kid looking in a toy store window.

Pulling on her hand, he gave her a wolfish grin and

raised his brows up and down. "Let's share the shower. Save time."

Twenty minutes later Tiffani stepped out on shaky knees from the most satisfying shower she had ever taken. Rex had sent her to the summit of ecstasy before he'd carefully bathed her then wrapped her in a towel. She was still floating on pleasure when she followed him in her car to his place.

"Let me get on something besides these day-old scrubs and I'll fix us something to eat." Rex was gone before she could answer.

She was outside, admiring his patio and garden, when Rex returned. He wore his usual T-shirt and jeans. His feet were bare. Tiffani had never seen a sexier sight. She had to get beyond this fascination with him.

"Would you like to eat out here?" he asked, joining her.

She fingered a plant. "That sounds wonderful."

"Then you enjoy the sunshine and I'll get us something to eat." He went inside.

Tiffani followed him.

"I thought you were going to stay outside." Rex looked up from where he was getting a frying pan out from underneath a cabinet.

"I'd rather watch you."

Rex grinned. "In that case, I'll try to put on a show."

He started by squirting oil into the pan with a couple of quick flicks of his wrist. Next he broke eggs with one hand while whipping them into a froth with the other. Tiffani wasn't only entertained but impressed. Was there nothing the man wasn't good at?

"This might be the best omelet I've ever eaten," she said a short while later as they sat across from each other at a café table tucked in a corner of the patio.

"That's the fresh herbs. Makes everything better. Eat up. We've got to go."

"You sure are excited about today." Tiffani forked into her eggs again.

"I rarely get a day that I just get to play. And to do it with a beautiful lady makes it extra-special."

That warm glow left over from the shower intensified again.

Half an hour later they were going to her car, again parked in his garage.

"Would you like to drive? It might give you more leg room," Tiffani suggested, offering him her keys.

"Sure. It's worth a try." He took them.

Soon they were on the interstate. Rex was whipping her car in and out of lanes as they sped down the road.

She held the handle of the door. "You do know this isn't a motorcycle?"

He grinned. "It's almost as good. Drives like a go-kart."

Tiffani put a hand on the edge of the seat. "Great. Now I'm riding with a daredevil."

"Just sit back and enjoy the ride," Rex said. "I've got this."

"I hope those won't be famous last words." She chuckled.

Rex pulled off onto a city street and his pace slowed.

"Are you a big Elvis fan?" Tiffani asked.

"Who isn't? But I'll have to admit I came to it later in life." Rex pulled into the parking lot across the road from Elvis's home, next to the large one-level museum. "How about you?"

"Yeah, I used to watch all his movies. Even sang along." She hadn't thought of that in a long time. She and her father had watched a number of them together.

As they were getting out of the car Rex asked, "You want to see everything? Museum, house and plane?"

Tiffani shrugged. "If we're here, we might as well."

He took her hand and gave it a squeeze. "That's the spirit. You're learning. After all, we're in no hurry."

"I do have to see my father this evening." The idea didn't hold much appeal.

"We can leave from here," Rex said, as they headed toward the ticket building.

That wasn't a good idea. She couldn't take Rex with her when she visited her father. "You don't have to do that. I'll have time to run you home."

"I'd like to meet your father."

She couldn't let that happen. "Didn't you hear me when I said he doesn't like doctors?"

Rex pulled her into his arms and gave her a quick kiss. "I believe you told me you didn't like doctors either. This morning in the shower you liked me pretty well, though, I thought."

She had. But just because she had changed her mind about one particular doctor it didn't mean it would make any difference to how her father felt about them. For certain he wouldn't like Rex even "pretty well" if he somehow found out Rex had spent the night with her.

"Come on, we can discuss that later. Elvis is waiting."

"Don't forget you agreed to pictures today." At Rex's snarl, she grinned.

He paid for their tickets and they entered the museum. They walked from one exhibit to another, watching videos of Elvis in concert, studying his cars, before they moved on to where one of his many costumes was on display behind glass.

"He dressed with flair," Tiffani commented.

Rex said as they looked at one display, "I remember my mom telling me about going to one of his concerts when she was a kid. She loved his music, still does. He would wipe sweat off with the bright colored scarf and throw it to the crowd. She got so excited when he came on stage, she made her way to within two rows of him, even though her seat wasn't anywhere near the front. A security guard finally told her to go back to her seat. She used to tell us that story all the time."

Done in the museum, they boarded a shuttle that took them across the road to Elvis's mansion. There they joined a small group of people waiting for a tour of the bottom floor of the house. Tiffani looked up at the tall columns of the brick antebellum-style house. "This had to be some place in its day."

When they were in the living room and the guide was telling them about the extra-long white sofa, Rex whispered in her ear, "I wish I had one like that. We'd have plenty of room."

Tiffani burned hot with memories and hissed, "Shh."

Rex grinned and hugged her close for a second. "By today's standards, this isn't all that large a place but at the time it must have been very impressive. Sitting up here on a hill with the white fence around it."

They strolled through the garden. Tiffani couldn't remember the last time she'd just walked hand in hand with a man with no real destination in mind. She really did need to let go more. Plan less, enjoy more. They worked their way to the area where Elvis and his parents were buried and stood there for a few moments.

"He really made his mark on the world, didn't he?" Tiffani said in a low voice.

"Yeah, he did." Rex kissed her cheek. "Not unlike what you have done in mine."

She looked at him in wonder. "Have I?"

"I'm riding around in a car, aren't I?"

"I guess I have." For some reason, that really mattered to her.

His smiling eyes met hers. "You've done more than that. It's been a long time since someone has been there for me like you were last night. Thank you."

"You are welcome." She couldn't resist kissing him.

They caught the shuttle back and went to visit Elvis's private plane. The day had been a perfect one so far and she couldn't think of anyone she'd rather be with than Rex. She was having *fun*. Something she had little of in her life.

The plane was decorated in the same style as the house, late nineteen-sixties and early seventies.

Taking a seat, Tiffani asked Rex, as if she were conducting an interview and he was Elvis, "So, what was your favorite movie part?"

"I liked *Girls, Girls, Girls*. Mostly because of the girls." Rex gave her a wolfish grin.

Tiffani laughed. "And your favorite song?"

"Oh, there were so many." Rex did a poor imitation of Elvis's voice. "'Blue Suede Shoes.'"

"Your favorite place in the world?"

"Graceland, of course."

They both giggled like kids.

Rex took her hand and helped her down the steps. "I heard that they have a café here that serves Elvis's favorite sandwich. Want to try it?"

"What is it?"

Rex rubbed his stomach. "A grilled peanut butter and banana sandwich."

Tiffani turned up her nose.

"Come on, Tiff, where's your sense of adventure?"

Put that way, she wasn't going to say no. "Okay, I'll give it a try."

They walked to the small café. Lining the walls were pictures of Elvis in his signature jumpsuits with rhinestones and a large collar. They found a table and a young waitress took their order.

Tiffani had to admire Rex. He was eager to try whatever came along. She'd spent so much of her life hesitating and questioning that it had never occurred to her she could live with fewer restrictions.

When their sandwiches were delivered Rex grabbed his and bit into it. He nodded at her. "It's really good."

She cut hers into quarters and picked up a section. Taking a tiny bite, she was pleasantly surprised. It was good.

"Told you so," Rex said, as he took another mouthful.

On the way to the car she said, "Thanks for bringing me. It really was a lot of fun."

"I'm glad we came too." In the car Rex turned to her. "What's the address to your dad's place?"

A knot of panic formed in Tiffani's stomach. She'd forgotten all about him saying he was going with her to visit her father. Somehow she had to convince him not to. "Why don't you just head to your place? You don't have to go with me. It really won't be pleasant."

"Surely it can't be that bad."

"You'd be surprised. Especially when he realizes you're a doctor." Why wouldn't Rex just accept she didn't want him to go?

"We just won't tell him. I'd like to meet him."

"Are you sure?" She didn't know how to keep him from going without hurting his feelings. Neither did she want her day with him to end. But visiting her father…

Rex met her look. "I'm sure. I'm a big boy. I can take care of myself."

"Head east on the interstate." Maybe she could convince Rex to wait in the lobby or car while she just checked in on her daddy. The closer they got to where her father lived, the more nervous she became. What if he recognized Rex?

He reached over and squeezed her hand. "It's going to be okay. I'll behave."

"It's not you I'm worried about. It's him." She knew how her father could act.

Rex pulled into a parking spot in front of the building. They walked together down the long hall. When Rex reached for her hand she pulled it back. Her father wouldn't like that. Rex didn't say anything but she felt more than saw his disapproval. Even so, it did feel good not to have to face her father alone for once.

She lightly knocked on the door. There was the expected growl of, "Come in."

"Hello, Daddy."

"Well, it's about time, baby girl."

Tiffani went farther into the room. "I brought somebody with me today."

Rex stepped up beside her and held out his hand. "Mr. Romano, I'm Rex. Nice to meet you."

"What'd you bring him for?" her father grumbled, ignoring Rex's proffered hand.

"He's a friend and wanted to meet you." She pulled a chair up close to her father and sat. "We've been to Graceland today."

"It's the middle of the week. You're not working on that awful campaign anymore? The one with the hospital?" he spat.

Alarm seized her. She had to steer the conversation in another direction. "Yes, but not today."

Her father twisted up his mouth. "I still can't believe you're such a traitor…"

Rex shifted behind her.

"How's your hand?" she said to change the subject. She could see the bandage needed replacing.

Her father raised it. "It hurts worse than ever."

"Did you let someone change it?" she asked automatically, suppressing a sigh of frustration.

"No," her father whined. "Only you do it right."

"Then let me change it." She went to the drawer where she stored supplies.

Rex couldn't believe what he'd just seen happen before his eyes. Tiffani had morphed into a child. Where was the tough PR woman he knew? The one who faced each of his complaints head on? It was like she was at her father's beck and call. Had she been taking care of her father for so long that she couldn't see the change? Tiffani had a big heart, but her father was taking advantage of her.

A loud intake of breath from Tiffani had him looking over her shoulder. Her father's hand was an angry red, with the look of infection setting in. He would require more help than a bandage.

"Daddy, have you told anyone how bad this is?" She glanced back at Rex.

"Why would I tell anyone? You were coming to see me. Maybe if you came more often it wouldn't have gotten so bad."

Rex was about to lose his patience. Nobody, not even her father, should talk to Tiffani that way. He went down on one heel beside her. "Let me have a look."

Tiffani continued to hold the man's hand in her palm while Rex examined it. It was going to require an antibiotic to keep the infection from spreading.

"What would you know about it?" her father snapped.

Rex looked him in the eyes. "I'm a doctor."

Mr. Romano reared up in his chair. "What? Get out of here! Get out of my room! Leave my daughter alone, you quack."

"Now, Daddy, he's only trying to help." Tiffani nudged him back down in the chair.

Rex hated to hear that placating tone in her voice.

"Doctors took my legs and now this one will probably want to take my hand," the old man ranted.

Rex stood and focused on Tiffani. "I'll wait for you outside."

"I'll only be a minute," she said over her shoulder.

Her father's face had turned red and he pointed toward the door. "Did you hear me? Get out! Leave my daughter alone."

Rex wanted to drag Tiffani away from the toxic man too. How had she lived with that hatred all these years? What must her childhood have been like? At least his parents hadn't taken out their pain at losing everything on him or his brother. Instead, they had worried about how their children were being affected.

He found one of the attendants and asked where to find the head of the nursing staff. Locating her, he identified himself and told her about Mr. Romano's hand, then called in a prescription for him. Rex was waiting in the lobby when Tiffani came down the hall, her shoulders slumped. The smiling and playful woman he'd known earlier in the day had disappeared. By the glisten of her eyes she was on the verge of tears. Rex put his arms around her and gave her a hug.

She buried her head in his chest. "I'm sorry. I should have insisted you not come in with me. He shouldn't have said those awful things to you."

"You warned me. Don't worry about it." He tightened his hold for a second before he said, "I called something in for him. His hand should be much better soon."

"That's if he takes it."

"The nurses around here know how to make that happen." He turned her toward the door. "Let's go home. We've had enough excitement for one day."

Tiffani looked at him. "Thank you."

"Not a problem." Where she was concerned, it wasn't.

CHAPTER NINE

BY THE TIME Rex had merged onto the interstate the sun was setting. "I didn't even think about the fact that we'd be driving into the sun this time of day."

"It does make it miserable and dangerous," Tiffani murmured.

They were the first words she'd said since getting into the car. Rex was glad she was coming out of the stupor that visiting her father had put her in. "You hungry? We could stop and get something."

"Not really. The sandwich filled me up."

He grinned at her. "It was good."

"I had a good time today. Thanks for making me play hooky."

"I had a good time with you today too." He took her hand and intertwined her fingers with his, lifting it with the intention of placing a kiss on her knuckles.

A bang filled the air.

"What the hell?" His look jerked to the road ahead.

Before him a car spun around. Another hit it and sent it into the path of a transfer truck. It flipped and rolled.

Tiffani released his hand and he quickly put it on the steering wheel. "Hold on." Glancing into the rearview mirror, he saw a car coming up on him fast. He whipped into the next lane. Slowing, he just missed the truck jack-knifing and came to a stop on the shoulder of the road.

"Do you have a flashlight in here?" he asked, already opening the door.

Tiffani didn't immediately answer.

"Tiffani!"

"Uh, it's in here." She unlatched the glove compartment and pulled out the light.

"I'm going to see who's hurt. Call 911 and report the accident. Tell them I'm here. Then I want you to find me. Don't get near any moving cars. Got that?"

"Yeah. Be careful. I don't want you to get hurt either," she called as he hurried away.

If they had been only a few seconds earlier it could be Tiffani and himself injured. His chest tightened. If he lost Tiffani… Had it come to that?

Debris covered the road. He almost tripped over a bumper. It had turned dark and this was the one stretch of road with little lighting. His first concern was the car that had rolled over.

Reaching it, he found a man struggling to get out. Rex went to his knees and shined the light on him. "I'm a doctor. Stay still, don't move any more than you have to. Help is on the way. How many people are in the car?"

"My wife. She's unconscious. My son and daughter are in the back." The man groaned.

Rex's chest constricted. Children. "I'll check on them. You stay still." He looked into the rear passenger window and was relieved to see two sets of wide eyes looking back at him.

Hurrying, he went around to the other side of the car. The door had been crushed. The woman's head was bleeding. Rex checked a pulse in her neck. It was faint but there. She needed medical attention right away.

Thankfully shrill sirens filled the air in the distance. A person came up behind him. "Can I help?"

"Yes. I'm a doctor. I want you to stay right here with this lady." Rex pointed to another person. "When the paramedics get here I want you to show them where this woman is. Do not move the people in the car. Understood?"

The people nodded.

Rushing to the next car, he passed the truck driver. He was wobbling on his feet. "Hey, buddy, you need to sit down." Rex shined the light on him. The man had a gash on his forehead.

"Rex, I'm here. What can I do?" Tiffani came to a halt beside him.

"I need you to get this man somewhere he can sit down and see if you can find something to put over the cut. I've got to check that other car."

He jogged in the direction of the second vehicle. There was no need to worry whether or not Tiffani would take care of the trucker. Rex was confident she would follow his instructions. At least this car was sitting upright. A middle-aged man sat behind the steering wheel. Rex tried the door handle. Tapping on the window, Rex said, "Open the door."

The man didn't look at him.

Was he in shock? Dead? Rex knocked harder at the window. "Sir, open the door."

The man looked at him through glazed eyes. There was a click of the lock. Rex pulled the door open. "Can you tell me what's wrong?"

Someone came up behind him. "Let me hold the flashlight."

It was Tiffani. He could count on her to know what

was needed. Handing it to her without looking back, he checked the man's pulse. It was erratic.

"Tiff, help me. We need to get him out of here. Go around to the other side and climb in. Help me get him out far enough that I can get him on the ground. I'm afraid he's headed for a heart attack."

Tiffani did as he instructed. She grunted in her effort to push the heavy man out of the seat. Finally Rex was able to get his arms under the man's shoulders and pull him from the vehicle. Tiffani rushed back around the car and held the light for him.

He could kick himself for not putting his emergency bag in Tiffani's car. Normally he had it on his bike. Placing his ear to the man's chest, he listened to his heartbeat and checked his pulse. It was unsteady, but there. The man needed immediate medical attention as well.

There wasn't enough of him to go around. Too many seriously injured. "Anyone here know CPR?" he asked the crowd behind him.

"I do," a woman said, coming forward.

"Then you stay here with this man. If he stops breathing you start CPR. I'll be right over there. You..." he pointed to a man "...go meet the paramedics and tell them they have a possible cardiac arrest. Tiffani, come with me."

Not asking any questions, she followed him. She stumbled, and he caught her before she went down. "Careful, I don't need you hurt too."

They returned to the woman in the first car. To his relief, the ambulance pulled up with lights flashing and sirens blaring.

"Tiffani, hold the light right there for me. I need to examine this woman." Rex placed his fingers on the artery in the woman's neck. All he was getting was a faint response. It was lighter than before. He felt over her chest to her midsection.

A brighter light than the one Tiffani was using shone over his shoulder, giving him a better view of the woman.

The paramedics came up behind him. He stood. "I'm Dr. Rex Maxwell. The best I can determine is that she has internal bleeding. Her husband and two children are in there as well. The man over there…" he pointed "…is having cardiac issues."

Tiffani stepped back from the car so as not to block the light. It turned out it was the light from a news camera.

A woman she recognized as a reporter at a local station came up beside her. "Who is that guy?"

For a second Tiffani didn't understand what the woman was talking about. "He's a doctor."

The reporter said, "We were only a few cars back when the accident happened, and started filming as soon as we got here. He's been amazing. A real hero."

Tiffani's mind shifted gears to her job. "That's Dr. Rex Maxwell, a surgeon at Metropolitan Hospital."

"He's been a lifesaver here tonight." Tiffani didn't miss the awe in the woman's voice.

As if on cue, Rex carried a child over to the ambulance and set him down. Tiffani glanced at the cameraman. He was focused on Rex and the camera was rolling. What would it hurt to give the newswoman a few choice tidbits about Rex? He might not like it but Tiffani still had a campaign to run. "Did you know he's the go-to general surgeon for west Tennessee? They find him indispensable over at the Metropolitan."

"Really?" The woman was obviously enthralled with Rex. "I'm going to have to get an interview with him."

A policeman approached and told them all to get out of the accident scene area. Tiffani was almost to the car when Rex jogged up.

"All the injured are going to Metro. I'm going to ride in with the woman. She'll need surgery right away. You good to get home by yourself?"

"Of course." She liked it that Rex worried about her but she'd been taking care of herself for a long time. "I'll be fine."

He gave her a quick kiss on the lips. "I'll call you."

Tiffani watched as he ran back into the thick of things. She couldn't help but be proud of him. He was her hero. And tomorrow he would be the city's.

Rex pulled his surgical cap off and dropped it into the bag hanging on a stand. It had been a long night. He'd been asked to scrub in when he'd arrived at the hospital. The woman had coded on the way in. It had taken everyone to keep her alive long enough to get her into the OR. There was a slim hope she'd make it through the night.

Now he was going to go home and get some sleep, then give Tiffani a call and invite her over for dinner. He smiled. And dessert. The sweet kind only she could provide.

"Hey, Rex, how does it feel to be the man of the hour? You hiding a red cape under those scrubs?" one of the doctors coming into surgery asked.

"Uh?"

He grinned even wider, "You haven't seen the news this morning, have you?"

"No, I've been in the OR until ten minutes ago. What're you talking about?" Rex was starting to get a nasty feeling in his gut.

"Go out in the waiting room and have a look at the

TV. They're even talking about you on social media. My wife texted me to see if I knew the doctor everyone was talking about."

Rex strode to the waiting room. Thankfully it was empty. He didn't have to wait to find out what was going on. There, in living color, was a video of him carrying the boy to the ambulance. He had offered to help and the paramedic had handed him the kid. The next clip was of him on his hands and knees beside the window of the other car involved. How had they gotten those pictures?

A knot formed in his chest. Anger roiled, feeding his suspicion. *Tiffani.* Would she do anything to get the publicity she needed? The picture moved to a woman holding a microphone, who was talking to Tiffani. She was talking about *him.* She had no excuse for not knowing how he would feel about taking advantage of the tragedy. How could she have done it? Because all she could think about was that promotion, about PR, about *appearances.* Just like his parents. Do whatever you can to get what you want, even if it hurts others.

Less than thirty minutes later he pulled his motorcycle in behind Tiffani's car parked in the driveway of her condo. Jerking his helmet off, he laid it on the seat and stomped to her door, not bothering with the bell, instead hammering on it. He didn't care who he woke.

Seconds later the lock clicked. Tiffani, dressed in her robe, opened the door and hissed, "What's wrong with you? It's early."

Rex pushed his way in and slammed the door behind him. He had to give her credit. She didn't even step back. "How could you? Does your job mean so much to you that you don't care about anyone else? Not even a family who almost lost a wife and mother?"

"You saw it?" She walked into the living area where her TV was turned to the morning news channel.

He followed on her heels. At least there was some contrition in her voice. "You bet I did. After I've spent hours in the OR, trying to save the woman's life, I came out to that nonsense."

"How is she?" Tiffani looked at him.

"Like you care."

She flinched. For a fleeting second he had compassion for her. He lowered his voice. "All you're interested in is getting your promotion. What did you do? Call the news?"

"They were already there. Not far behind us on the road. The reporter came up to me. They had already been filming you. I just told them your name and where you worked."

His eyes bored into hers. "And you knew good and well how I'd feel about that."

"I had an idea, but it was too good an opportunity to pass up, Rex. You *were* a hero last night. If you hadn't helped those people, they could have died."

"You're just like my parents. Trying to dress things up to look a certain way when they're not. I'm a doctor, I care for people. That's my job. My calling. I don't do it so I can be a hero on the morning news. Don't make me into something I'm not."

She put her hands out, palms up as if pleading with him. "But the coverage was important—"

"Why? So you can get a promotion and run away from a jerk who was never good enough for you to begin with?" he spat.

"Run away?" She made a step toward him. "You're one to be talking. You run every day from who you were. You did a complete role reversal so you don't have to re-

member how much it hurt to be rejected from your old
life. And you're blaming everyone else for feeling that
way. I bet you don't even see your parents but maybe
once a year! Yet, from all I can tell, outside of them
trying to live the good life, they loved you. They cared
for you."

"Don't put your issues on me just because you act like
this strong, assertive woman, but when you get around
your father you become a child who'll do anything to
make him happy. The problem is you *can't*. He uses his
disability to control you. You can't see he's eaten up
with bitterness and that if you don't get away soon, one
day you will be too."

Her shoulders reared back as if he had slapped her.
"How dare you!"

"I dare because it's the truth. Have you ever thought
that he might have learned to walk on artificial legs if
you hadn't waited on him hand and foot? He demanded
attention. You gave it to him. You're still giving it.
Granted, you were a child, but he should've been man
enough to know better than to put that guilt trip on you.
All that stuff about doctors is to cover up his fault in the
accident. You ask him. I bet he was driving too fast. Had
been drinking. Not paying attention to the road. You and
I both know his doctors saved his life."

"If you're done psychoanalyzing me and my father,
you need to go." Tiffani circled around him and got as
far from him as the space would allow. She held the
door wide.

He gave her a pointed look. "I'm going, but I won't
be anyone's pawn. I am through with your crusade. I'll
let Nelson know. You do your thing without me. Goodbye, Ms. Romano."

CHAPTER TEN

REX'S FINAL WORDS had rerun over and over in her mind like a bad film for days. He'd called her by her last name. When he'd said goodbye that was what he'd meant. Not only to the campaign but to her. She'd thought she'd been hurt before by a breakup but that pain came nowhere near the searing agony she was feeling now. Just getting out of bed was torture. The only relief she found was sleep but there was precious little of that. The dreams were too intense. She woke aching for Rex. It was both a pleasure and a pain to see his smiling face on the billboards around town.

Dr. Nelson had called the next day to inform her Rex would no longer be required to participate in the campaign. She had no idea how Rex had explained the situation and she hadn't asked. Despite Dr. Nelson's announcement, he seemed genuinely pleased with her progress. That news coverage of the accident scene had boosted the hospital's image in the public's eyes—and destroyed any chance she had at happiness.

She had fallen in love with Rex.

But she had hurt him. Worse, disappointed him. She couldn't take it back. Didn't know how to fix it. All she knew to do was accept the promotion she had been of-

fered for her successful campaign, move away and hope
to start anew. There would never be another Rex. Just a
hole in her heart where the piece he held belonged. Had
he been right to accuse her of running away by chasing
the promotion to the other office? She'd never thought
of herself as a coward. If she could endure losing Rex,
then she shouldn't have any difficulty facing Lou every
day at work. After all, she *did* deserve better than him.
She'd let Lou treat her like her father did. That wasn't a
healthy relationship. For a boyfriend or a father. It was
time to make changes in her life.

That Sunday when she visited her father she entered
his room with her head held high. It was time for him
to start taking responsibility for his actions and his life.

"Baby girl. There you are."

She didn't pull up a chair. Instead she chose to stand.
"Hi, Daddy. How's your hand?"

He waved it at her. He no longer wore a bandage.
"Much better. Even though that quack looked at it."

"You're not going to talk about Rex that way around
me. If you do I won't be coming to see you anymore,"
she said tightly, holding her father's shocked gaze.

"But you know how those doctors are."

She did. The one she loved was giving, caring and
dedicated. "Daddy, you never really told me what caused
your accident."

Her father looked uncomfortable and turned his gaze
away from her. "Why do you want to know now? That
was a long time ago."

"It was but I'd still like to know." She used her most
encouraging tone.

"I was on the way home from work. I came through

a curve and the bike came out from under me." He repeated the words as if it was a rehearsed statement.

"You didn't stop on the way home? You used to tell me you stopped by Charlie's for a drink sometimes." She watched him closely. His eyes shadowed.

"I might have. I don't really remember."

Tiffani could tell he did. "It had been raining that day."

"How do you know that?" he said with uncharacteristic quietness.

"Because I couldn't go out to play. I ran to the door when the policeman rang the bell."

"Ah." He nodded, still not meeting her look.

Rex had been right. There was more to the story than what her father wanted to admit to.

"Dad, I think it's time you think about getting some help. Use your wheelchair more. Get outside some. Talk to other people."

There was moisture in his eyes. "What's going on?"

"It's time for you to take responsibility for yourself. I'm not going to enable you anymore. I'm not coming to see you for a while. I think we both need a little time to think."

"That's fine with me. I don't need you," he spat.

"Bye, Dad." She sighed. "I'll see you in a few weeks."

Tiffani walked down the hall with her shoulders straight but that had been one of the hardest things she had ever done. She'd hated to do it but it had needed to be done. She and her father needed space from one another.

Tiffani stopped by the attendants' desk and told the woman there, "I just wanted to let you know I won't be coming in for a while. My dad needs to learn to deal with things on his own."

The woman gave her a wry smile. "I couldn't agree more."

"Thanks for taking care of his hand. It looks much better," Tiffani said.

"It does. I told Dr. Maxwell that as well just yesterday."

Rex had been checking in on her father? Even after the way her father had treated him?

"Bye," she told the woman, and hurried out of the building before she broke down in sobs.

Rex had worked himself to the point of exhaustion for over a week now. That was the only way he could get any sleep. Still, those hours weren't restful ones. He missed Tiffani. The worst thing he could have ever done was invite her up to his place. Now, wherever he looked he thought of her, even when washing his clothes.

As soon as he had made it home that morning after seeing Tiffani, he had phoned Nelson. He was excited about the TV report but his joy vanished when Rex told him in no uncertain terms that he wouldn't be continuing as part of the PR campaign. If the hospital didn't want him for his skills he would go elsewhere. Nelson assured him the hospital didn't want to lose him. When he asked what the problem was, Rex just told him that he and Ms. Romano could no longer agree on how much of his time could be diverted from surgery for the sake of the campaign.

He felt betrayed. She'd chosen her career over him. Once again, someone he cared about had placed their own wants and needs ahead of anything else.

His job was to help people, not create material for

great PR. He'd done his best by Mr. Royster and it had come back to bite him. He was trying to do the right thing for the people in the High Water neighborhood, but what if somehow that turned into a negative too? He hoped not. Surely Tiffani wouldn't use the clinic like that.

But now, after calming down, he couldn't help but wonder if she had been right. Was he doing the same thing as she was? Running? He wouldn't have ever believed he was doing that, but now…

Were his hair, clothes and motorcycle all a show? How was his determination to present a specific image to the world any different from what his parents had done? They'd worn clothes for who they wanted to be, had lived the lifestyle they'd wanted. Where they had messed up had been failing to create a plan to prevent it all from one day crashing down on them. Was his blind determination to be an individual with no pretensions causing him to push away the one person he wanted in his life?

Tiffani had been right. His parents loved him. They had cared about him when he'd been a child and even now they called regularly. He just hadn't returned the same treatment. They had asked for his forgiveness but he had yet to give it. They'd made a mistake, but their family had survived. What had he really lost? Nothing except a girl who he'd learned cared more about money and appearances than she did him. That wasn't a bad thing to know before it was too late.

He'd accused Tiffani of doing the same thing, but she'd abided by his request to keep the clinic out of the media. She could have used it. More than once he'd given her the opportunity to use her knowledge of him personally for the sake of the campaign, but she hadn't.

She'd explained what had happened at the accident. The question was, did he believe her? But why shouldn't he? Tiffani hadn't lied to him before.

What had he done? He'd overreacted. Lost the most wonderful thing that had ever happened to him. She brought out the best in him.

Tiffani had opened her arms wide and taken him in when he'd needed her that terrible night. There had been no questions or condemnation, just a warm, safe harbor for his wounded soul. Even when he'd told her about what his parents had done, she'd seen the positive side. Pointed out what they had done right. Tiffani knew how to care and what had he shown her? Disdain. Scorn.

Shame filled him. He'd spent much of his adult life acting holier than thou. The very thing he despised. It was time to apologize. His parents were first on his list. Then with his heart in his hand he was going to ask Tiffani for forgiveness.

And pray hard she would give it.

Two days later, Rex gathered enough courage to call his parents and ask if he could visit. His mother sounded both surprised and overjoyed to hear from him. That weekend he showed up at their house on Saturday morning. He hadn't even pulled very far into the drive before his mother and father came out to greet him.

As he put his helmet on the seat his mother embraced him with a hug and a kiss on the cheek. "Honey, this is a real treat. We're so glad to see you."

His father gave him a bear hug, bringing Rex in close and gently pounding on his back. Guilt washed over him. All these years he'd been pushing his parents away with his attitude, and by refusing to see them more. Tiffani had faithfully visited her father regularly for all her adult life and had probably never once received the warm reception Rex just had. He promised himself he would do better about being a part of his parents' lives.

"Come in and tell us all about what you have been doing." His mother wrapped her arm around his and walked close as they entered the house.

It was nothing like the one Rex had grown up in. Where his childhood home had been spacious and two stories with a pool in the back, this one was bungalow-sized and in an established blue-collar area of the city. Just big enough for two. He had to give them credit for trying to live within their means. Even their car was a basic four-door and secondhand, from the looks of it.

His mother led them into the kitchen. The table was laid with his favorite meal. "You know I'm not much of a cook, but I tried."

Rex gave her a hug. "It looks wonderful, Mom. Thanks."

Her father chuckled. "She's been working and worrying since you called."

There was something to be said for being loved. Rex hadn't realized what he'd had until he'd seen Tiffani's father in action.

They took seats at the table and chatted about what was going on in their lives and his brother's while they ate.

Then, as if his mother couldn't stand it any longer, she blurted out, "Tell us about that billboard."

"You saw that," Rex said, his appetite dying.

"Hard to miss." His father chuckled.

His mother's gaze met his. "I was surprised. I never thought you'd agree to anything like that."

"The person who talked me into it can be pretty

persuasive." Rex went on to explain his involvement in the campaign.

Both his parents looked at him, amazed.

"I knew the Royster business must have taken a toll on you but you never said anything, and, to be truthful, I felt responsible," his father said.

"You weren't. His family just didn't want to accept the truth," Rex assured him.

His mother's eyes held a sad look. "We should've been more supportive during that time but we were afraid we'd make it worse."

"It might have. I know I've been hard on you about what happened years ago. I was a kid only thinking about himself. I just want you to know that I'm grateful for your love. More than that, I appreciate you loving each other. Even though you've lived through tough times, you stuck together. You loved us. That's to be admired. I've always known you were there for me, even when I didn't show it."

His mother was openly crying and his father had moisture in his eyes. His mother said between sobs, "We thought you'd never forgive us."

"Thank you for telling us that. May I ask why you told us this now?" his father asked.

Rex gave him a direct look. "A woman."

His father nodded sagely. "That'll do it."

There was a sparkle of interest Rex hadn't seen in his mother's eyes in a long time. "When do we get to meet her?"

"Soon, I hope. I have some groveling to do first."

"It's like that, is it?" his father said with a grin.

"Yeah, I messed up."

"We all do that sometimes," his mother whispered, wiping her eyes.

"It has taken me too long to figure that out. For that I'm deeply sorry," Rex said, looking at his mother then his father.

As he was leaving his mother asked, "When're you going to get rid of that motorcycle? It scares me."

"Soon. I think it's time I make some changes in my life."

Tiffani stepped out of the taxi in front of the historic Peabody Hotel in downtown Memphis. She had chosen to come by taxi so she didn't have to worry about finding a parking place or waiting in line for a valet. She'd delayed dressing to the last minute, unsure if she wanted to even attend the cocktail party and dinner being held for the visiting accreditation committee.

Dr. Nelson had called and left a message at her office that she was invited to attend. She'd spent most of the last week and a half working on the campaign from a distance. She'd had numerous requests to interview Rex but she had declined them all. She wasn't going to ask and he wasn't going to agree.

She hadn't spoken to or seen her father since her last visit. Unable to stand it, she had called the home and asked the nurse how he was doing. She'd been told her father had become increasingly difficult the first few days after her last visit but that he was more agreeable now. The nurse assured Tiffani she had done a good thing by making her father face a few facts.

Tonight Tiffani had dressed in a light blue dress she saved for special occasions. It fit well and she felt she looked good in it. Not that she would see anyone that mattered. Rex would certainly not be there. This type of dinner wasn't his thing. She'd left her hair down and pulled it over to one side. Wearing it free was a habit now. Rex had been right. She had dressed to appear unapproachable. After Lou had dumped her she'd hidden behind her appearance, her job. Now she knew well what it was like to have a man truly appreciate who she was. The sad part was that she'd lost him, but she refused to let the lessons she'd learned about herself be overshadowed by negativity.

The time of the cocktail party had been arranged so that everyone attending could enjoy the Duck March beforehand. Twice a day, live ducks and their offspring, who had been trained in a unique tradition, trooped dutifully into the lobby of the hotel and swam in the beautiful lobby fountain. She'd seen it when she was a child but not recently. It would give her something to smile about, something she hadn't done since Rex had walked out her door. There was already a crowd forming along the red carpet stretching from the elevators to the fountain in the center of the lobby. All of this to watch five mallard ducks walk to a fountain for a swim.

Tiffani found an open spot near the fountain. A few minutes later the doors to the ornate elevator opened and out walked the ducks, followed by the Duckmaster. She couldn't help but grin.

"They're fun, aren't they?" a voice she knew well said from behind her. *Rex*.

Tiffani's insides quaked. He was here! And talking to her. "They are. I love them."

The ducks waddled past them on their way into the fountain.

Rex came to stand beside her, just touching. It was like the sun burning brightly along that side of her body. He wore a dark suit and shirt and a conservative striped tie. The only omission to looking like a professional in the traditional sense was his hair. The edge that had al-

ways drawn her to him was still there, making her glow
hot in her middle.

The ducks swam a couple of laps in a circle, climbed
out of the fountain, shook off and gathered to make the
march back.

Rex whispered in her ear close enough his breath
brushed her hair. "Can we talk?"

Tiffani tingled all over. This was her chance to tell
him how she felt. She'd made the mistake of trying to
share her heart with the wrong person once, but she had
no doubt Rex was the man for her. She met his gaze.
"Please. I'd like that."

Dr. Nelson said, passing them with a group of people,
"Hey, you two. We're going to the Rooftop Bar."

"We'll be along in a few minutes," Rex said, taking
her hand and heading in the other direction.

Hope flared in Tiffani. "Maybe we should—"

"We have more important things to do," Rex said,
hurrying her toward the lavish lobby stairs. He started
up them.

"Where are we going?"

"You'll see." At the top he guided her along the hall,
turned right at the end and a few rooms down stopped
in front of a door. Putting the key in the lock, he opened
the door wide.

"You were that sure of me?" Tiffani didn't try to hide
her suspicious tone.

His eyes took on a worried look. Was he anxious?
Fearful she might reject him? She couldn't think of a
time she'd ever seen Rex anything but confident. Even
when he'd been upset, having done all he could have
for a patient.

"No, I was that hopeful. And we needed a quiet place

to talk. You don't have to come in if you don't want to. And you're free to leave anytime you wish."

"I think I'll take my chances." Tiffani smiled and saw the tension in his shoulders ease.

She stepped to the middle of the room. It was decorated in a pale green. The walls, the window treatments, the carpet and the bedding were all a variation on the color, giving the space an elegant look. A large four-poster bed was the center of attention but there was a small sitting area near one window.

"Wow, this is a beautiful room. I've always wondered what one of the rooms at the Peabody looked like."

Rex shrugged out of his jacket and walked to the sitting area, where he put it over the back of the small sofa. He loosened his tie and said, "Why don't we sit? I need to say something to you."

He didn't touch her when she went past him. She took one of the two chairs and Rex sat on the settee, facing her.

"I have something I want to say first," Tiffani said.

"My meeting, I go first."

She sank back in her chair and put her hands in her lap. "All right."

"I owe you an apology."

That wasn't at all what she'd expected.

"For how I acted about the accident being on TV," he continued. "I know you were only doing your job. I trust you, and know you were telling me the truth about what happened. I've been so wrapped up in trying not to be who I used to be, I forgot to appreciate who I am now."

Tiffani began to say something.

He put up a hand. "I'm not finished eating humble pie. I want to thank you for making me see what kind of parents I really have. I've let one part of their personalities overshadow everything about them, including the good. I went to see them the other day and told them how much I appreciate them." He relaxed and watched her.

She waited for a few seconds. "May I talk now?"

He grinned. "Please do, before you explode."

"I want to thank you. Because of you, I now see what my father was doing to me. How I was enabling him. I told him I wouldn't be back to see him until he decided to take responsibility for himself. And about the accident being on the news, I'm sorry I hurt you. I didn't intend to. I let the thought of a promotion get in the way. But it wasn't worth losing you over."

"You haven't lost me." Rex went down on one knee in front of her and took her hands. "I was afraid you wouldn't forgive me."

Raw emotion as sweet as spring water flowed from Tiffani. She cupped his face. "That would never happen."

"I love you."

She had no doubt he did. "I love you too."

Rex lay back on the pillows piled against the headboard with Tiffani securely in his arms. He kissed her temple. His need for her had overwhelmed him to the point that talking was no longer possible. They had unfinished business. His future was with her and he needed to secure it.

"Shouldn't we be thinking about going to the dinner? Dr. Nelson will miss us," she murmured as she ran a hand over his chest.

"I don't care if he does. I had more fun here with just you."

"That was a nice thing to say. Speaking of nice things,

I meant to tell you how handsome you looked in your suit. You cut a dashing figure." She grinned.

"Don't get too used to me dressing that way."

Tiffani gave him one of those smiles he had missed so much.

"So have you heard anything about that promotion?" He needed to know. If she was moving he would be going with her, if she would have him. He would start his career over wherever she was.

"I got it." Excitement filled her voice.

Rex was both glad and sad. He was pleased for her but he hated to leave his practice.

She was quick to say, "But I got a better offer today." Dared he hope?

She was already explaining. "Dr. Nelson wants me to come on board as the head of the Metropolitan's PR department. He was so impressed with the campaign he said he couldn't let me go."

"Is that what you want? I'll go wherever you are." He meant it. Life without Tiffani would be intolerable.

"That's the nicest thing anyone has ever offered to do for me, but I couldn't take you from the hospital or the clinic." She gave him a teasing smile. "And all your fans. The billboard company said your picture has been the most successful they have ever had."

"Yeah." There was no note of enthusiasm in his voice. "At least I have some claim to fame."

She kissed him. "You'll always be the most wonderful person to me."

"And you to me." He held her tight, secure in the knowledge he would never let her go.

* * * * *

MILLS & BOON

Coming next month

BOUND BY THEIR BABIES
Caroline Anderson

People joked all the time about sex-crazed widows, and there was no way—*no way*—she was turning into one! This was *Jake*, for heaven's sake! Her friend. Not her lover. Not her boyfriend. And certainly not someone for a casual one-nighter.

Although they'd almost gone there that once, and the memory of the awkwardness that had followed when they'd come to their senses and pulled away from the brink had never left her, although it had long been buried.

Until now…

Emily heard the stairs creak again, and pressed down the plunger and slid the pot towards him as he came into the room.

'Here, your coffee.'

'Aren't you having any?'

She shook her head, but she couldn't quite meet his eyes, and she realised he wasn't looking at her, either. 'I'll go back up in case Zach cries and wakes Matilda. Don't forget to ring me when you've seen Brie.'

'OK. Thanks for making the coffee.'

'You're welcome. Have a good day.'

She tiptoed up the stairs, listened for the sound of the front door closing and watched him from his bedroom window as he walked briskly down the road towards the hospital, travel mug in hand.

He turned the corner and went out of sight, and she sat down on the edge of his bed, her fingers knotting in a handful of rumpled bedding. *What was she doing?* With a stifled scream of frustration, she fell sideways onto the mattress and buried her face in his duvet.

Mistake. She could smell the scent of him on the sheets, warm and familiar and strangely exciting, could picture that glorious nakedness stretched out against the stark white linen, a beautiful specimen of masculinity in its prime—

She jack-knifed to her feet. This was crazy. What on earth had happened to her? They'd been friends for years, and now all of a sudden this uncontrollable urge to sniff his sheets?

They had to keep this platonic. So much was riding on it—their mutual careers, if nothing else!

And the children—they had to make this work for the children, especially Matilda. The last thing she needed—any of them needed—was this fragile status quo disrupted for anything as trivial as primitive, adolescent lust.

It wasn't fair on any of them, and she'd embarrassed herself enough fifteen years ago. She wasn't doing it again.

No way.

Continue reading
BOUND BY THEIR BABIES
Caroline Anderson

Available next month
www.millsandboon.co.uk

LET'S TALK

Romance

For exclusive extracts, competitions
and special offers, find us online:

f facebook.com/millsandboon

⦿ @millsandboonuk

𝕭 @millsandboon

Or get in touch on 0844 844 1351*

For all the latest titles coming soon, visit
millsandboon.co.uk/nextmonth

Want even more
ROMANCE?

Join our bookclub today!

'Mills & Boon books, the perfect way to escape for an hour or so.'

Miss W. Dyer

'Excellent service, promptly delivered and very good subscription choices.'

Miss A. Pearson

'You get fantastic special offers and the chance to get books before they hit the shops'

Mrs V. Hall